T0146599

UNBLEMISHED

The Romance of Imperfection

Lily Cameron had learned to live with the
birthmark blemish on her face, but could she
live with the blemish on the soul of the man she loved?
Or with those who wanted to
destroy them both?

CHRISTOPHER SHENNAN

UNBLEMISHED
THE ROMANCE OF IMPERFECTION

iUniverse books may be ordered through booksellers or by contacting:

iUniverse
1663 Liberty Drive
Bloomington, IN 47403
www.iuniverse.com
1-800-Authors (1-800-288-4677)

ISBN: 978-1-5320-3529-6 (sc)
ISBN: 978-1-5320-3530-2 (e)

Print information available on the last page.

iUniverse rev. date: 10/28/2017

INTRODUCTION

This book is fiction, in that the characters and the situations they find themselves in are the product of the author's imagination. Any resemblance to any situations and living individuals is entirely co-incidental.

The central truth, however, that this fictional story is based upon is not fiction, but the plain truth gleaned from the pages of the Bible, God's Living Word.

The sins and blemishes of the human condition can and will be removed for anyone who understands and receives the Gospel of Christ in sincerity and truth. I have unapologetically quoted Scripture throughout to support the central idea: God *does* forgive sinners, and He *does* remove the blemish of sin from the human spirit.

Acknowledgements

I acknowledge that without the Presence of the Triune God in my life, this book would not have been written. I give God all the glory for any excellence of style and presentation that may be found in it; I take full responsibility for anything that falls short of both spiritual and literary standards.

There are others, however, that deserve to be mentioned:

Allison Legendre, the artist who illustrated the cover of this book, deserves my gratitude.

Paul Speer, a very valued friend and brother in Christ, has provided invaluable support. He read the manuscript beforehand to make sure the book was indeed worth publishing. I am gratified he placed his seal of approval upon it.

Doris Kull took away from a very busy life to ensure the manuscript was ready for publication.

I thank Mike Skinner for the many private debates we have engaged in. They served to sharpen my understanding of Scripture.

Words fail me to describe the contribution my wife, Pamela Joyce Shennan made to the development and completion of this book. She had to endure endless sharing of my ideas over the dinner table and in private discussions. At first she was only able to read it in bits and pieces while the book was being written, but added proof-reading to her many contributions. To you, Pamela I give my heartfelt thanks, and my love.

CONTENTS

Prologue

Winter 1967- St Catharines Ontario, Canada

Angus Cameron looked up from his Bible reading and fixed his attention on his seven year old daughter, Lily. She was playing with her doll on the living room carpet at her mother's feet. The sight caused a tightening in his throat.

She was sitting so all he could see was her left profile, her right toward her mother. What he was seeing was the loveliest picture of youthful beauty imaginable, and it was not just the prejudice of parental love that told him so. Such perfection of face and form could only have come as a blessing from above, and the natural beauty inherited from her mother. She had the same golden highlights in her dark blonde, shoulder-length hair, exquisitely shaped cheeks and Cupid's bow lips. He knew her eyes were the same sky blue intensity and her form held the promise of future feminine curves that would be the envy of all her girlfriends.

Her mother was slowly losing those perfections to the ravages of cancer, but they were living again in the daughter playing quietly at her feet.

Lily held up her doll so that the light from the table lamp shone fully on its features, and his throat tightened again. Lily had used her markers to create a wine coloured blemish on the doll's cheek, a passable replica of the one she bore on her own right cheek.

As if to demonstrate this Lily turned and presented her right side to her father's view, and there on that perfect face, was the birthmark covering her entire cheek down to the curve of her jaw – a blemish on what would have been perfect beauty. The expression in Lily's eyes, as she rose and came to cuddle on her father's lap, held no shadow of that blemish. Angus, and his God, had helped to remove it from her soul.

Angus remembered, two years ago, when Lily had come to him with a question after playing with the little girl next door, "Daddy, why did God blot my face?" She touched her fingers to her blemished cheek, "Angela doesn't have one like I have."

Angus could only attribute divine wisdom and inspiration to what had followed. He had held her at arms-length and looked deeply into her eyes, "Lily, God has given you a special mark that other little girls do not have."

"Why, Daddy?"

"To mark you out for special blessings. He wants you to remember where true beauty lies. It is not in beauty of face and form. It is in an unblemished person on the inside." He had had to explain to her then, and since, what "unblemished" meant, but she had been an avid pupil.

A light of understanding spread over her face and lit up her eyes, "How do I become un...?"

"Unblemished."

Umbwemished on the inside, Daddy?

"I will teach you, Lily. The Lord Jesus and I will teach you," was what he had said.

CHAPTER ONE

The Stare

Spring 1980

Lily's best friend, Heather Rawlings, regarded her across the coffee house table with something approaching incomprehension, "I just can't figure you out, Lily Cameron. You're twenty years old, with a body to die for, and guys ready to line up for the privilege of taking you out, and you won't even consider going out with *any* of them."

"I'm just not into dating, Heth, plain and simple. Besides, even if I did date, it would have to be someone who loves the Lord like I do."

"Lil, there are several guys at church who love the Lord whom I know like you – a lot."

"Good to have as friends," Lilly said, "nothing more."

"Wow! You're really picky. You know that?"

"Better to be picky than to marry the wrong guy."

"So, you haven't ruled out marriage altogether, then?"

"Of course not. I believe the Lord has the right one for me – in His time."

Heather sighed, "If I looked like you and had fellas interested in me, I'd sure would go out with them to help me decide. If you don't date, how're you going to know who the right one is?

Lily gave her friend a searching look, "Heather, why are we even having this discussion. We're best friends and you know what I believe. I'll know the right man for me when I meet him."

Heather let go of her coffee cup she had apparently been squeezing the life out of, and leaned back. Her tone when she spoke again had changed to one of resignation, "You get these ideas from your father, don't you?"

Lily was aware Heather thought she was too much influenced by her father, and felt she had to start thinking for herself. Truthfully, she put great stock in her father's perspective on life. Ever since her mother had died of cancer when she was ten, the bond between them had become stronger. He had taught her life principles she was convinced had saved her from many of the pitfalls that plague young women in their teen years. She realized the blemish on her face might have caused a blemish on her soul, had he not focused her attention on inner beauty rather than outward appearance.

Gazing fondly at her friend, Lily thought how attractive she was in her own way. She could not be described exactly as beautiful, but her auburn hair framed pleasant features, and her brown eyes were vibrant and expressive. Any young man with eyes to see would find qualities in Heather that would endure. She was fiercely loyal to her friends, and had a sweetness of temperament that would last long after wrinkles and age-spots had changed her youthful appearance.

Lily had often thought how much simpler her own life would be if she did not have what Heather called, "a body to die for." Heather's unspectacular looks would have suited her very nicely, thank you.

Lily answered her friend's question carefully, aware she had not meant to be critical of her father, "Heth, Daddy has taught me a lot, even most of what I believe, but I have not blindly followed his advice – at least not since I was quite young. He encouraged me to test his ideas by the searchlight of Scripture, common sense, and by observing life first-hand. I have learned a lot from Daddy, and am grateful for what he has taught me, but I have come to my own conclusions. I believe what I believe because of my own relationship with Jesus, and not just because of what he told me."

"But he *has* influenced you."

"Doubtless, but there are all kinds of influences out there, Heather. If we don't carefully choose what influences we allow to give our lives direction, we may end up at the wrong destination. We both know people who have just 'gone with the flow' and ended up in trouble. I choose Daddy's influence over most of what I see leading young people astray today."

"I suppose you are right, Lily," Heather sighed, "Most of the time you are anyway. I just find myself wishing special things for you. I see the clock ticking and you don't even have a boyfriend."

"By choice, Heather, and twenty is not old."

"No, but time flies, and you could find yourself an old maid in the blink of an eye."

Lily sensed the conversation was about to go around in circles, so she rose and asked, "Another coffee?"

"Sure," Heather answered, her mouth set in a good natured pout. It was her habitual expression when she felt she had lost an argument to Lily.

As she stood in line, Lily glanced out the window at Welland Ave, her memory following till it reached Cushman, and then to the Welland Canal, that famous shipping lane that carried freight and pleasure boats through from Port Weller to Port Colborne. She knew the canal formed a key section of the St. Lawrence Seaway, enabling ships to ascend and descend the Niagara Escarpment and bypass Niagara Falls, and eventually out to sea.

The canal was just one familiar part of her beloved St. Catharines. This was *her* city. Though it was small with only 132,000 population compared to Hamilton, fifty kilometers away with over half a million, it was the perfect balance between small and large. It was big enough to have all the conveniences of a large city – you could obtain almost anything you wanted without having to order from elsewhere – It was small enough to exclude some of the seedier elements of bigger cities.

And the QEW, or Queen Elizabeth Way, made a division between the North Side and the South Side of St. Catharines, giving easy access to any part of the city you wanted to go...

"May I help you, miss?" the young man behind the counter asked.

Returning from her reverie, she placed her order and carried the coffee back to her friend. The server had not been able to stop staring at the birthmark on her right cheek. She had learned to interpret these looks and she could guess at what he was thinking. His expression said, "What a shame. Such a beautiful girl and what an ugly mark on her face. I wonder why she doesn't have it removed."

Lily registered the shock, the surprise, and even the pity directed at her on meeting people she had never met before, but it failed to bother

her, at least not greatly. This was her special mark, and while she did not enjoy this kind of attention, she accepted it as her lot in life. She refused to allow it to rob her of her self-worth. God had made her this way, and it was all part of His special plan for her life. Her father, Angus Cameron, had taught her that, and she embraced his guidance completely. She had seen the results in those who allowed their outward imperfections to twist them on the inside.

This was not to say she had not struggled with negative reactions to what people regarded as a 'pitiful blemish', but at twenty years old she had fought all those battles, and won. She would trust and not be afraid of what the future held for her.

Lily rejoined Heather and they sat in companionable silence, till Heather surprised her by brightly asking, "So what kind of romance do you think God will send your way?"

Lily gave her friend an astonished look, "I have absolutely *no* idea. Now Heather, can't we just talk about something else? It makes me uncomfortable."

"Alright. What shall we talk about, Lil?"

"How about your own plans for college. Or, since you've been fixated on my romantic interest, or lack of them, we should talk about your *own* romantic future."

Heather blushed all shades of pink, "What romantic future? I don't have any."

"Come now Heth, you're a healthy young woman with natural longings, and I've seen your secret glances at a certain young man at church."

"You mean Luke?" She made a dismissive sound in her throat, "He doesn't even know I exist. Now if I looked a bit more like…"

Lily held up her hand in a halting gesture, "Now stop it dear friend. You've got yourself into an unhealthy way of thinking."

"How so?"

"You've become blind to your own qualities and imagine only girls of a certain type will attract a man. God has made you the way you are. Besides being really pretty, you have character. I've never known such a loyal friend. You're kind, considerate, and your love for the Lord's work, and children is recognized by everyone."

"You think I'm pretty, Lil? Heather asked doubtfully.

"You have the most beautiful expressive eyes I have ever seen."

"A lot of good that will do if Luke doesn't get close enough to look into them. I don't have a figure like you have, more straight up and down."

Lilly sighed in frustration, "What am I going to do with you, Heth? You may not have the 'Barbie-doll look, but you're attractive all the same. Besides, Luke may just be shy. He may just not know how to express his interest."

They moved on to other subjects and settled into that comfortable interaction that best friends all over the world enjoy – until Lily became aware of a prickly sensation on her right cheek. Prickly was the best word she could describe it, for it was not physical. It was more of an instinctive awareness. She turned to find a pair of pale green eyes from a few tables away fixed on her. She quickly looked away, an odd sensation passing through her, causing her heart to beat more rapidly.

Heather noticed the quick intake of her breath and touched her fingers to Lily's arm, "What's the matter, Lil?"

"Er... nothing. No, that's not quite true. I caught someone staring at me."

Heather sighed, "Lil, people are always staring it you, at one time or another, either because of the birthmark on your cheek, or your stunning good looks. It's never bothered you before. Is he, I assume it is a he, staring at your cheek? I refuse to call it a blemish."

"Yes, and it is a man, and he's not staring *at* my birthmark. You'll think I'm crazy. He's staring *through* it."

"Who is it?"

"You can see him better than I can – two tables behind us, across the aisle. Brown hair, in a green jacket."

"Oh, oh," Heather breathed, "of all the men you could decide to notice, you have to pick *him*."

Against her will, Lily found herself turning to look at the stranger. As she did so their eyes locked and a jolt went through her, robbing her of speech, and the power to breathe. Lily had never experienced a connection with another human being as she did with this man she had never before met – not even her own father. It was as if their eyes provided a conduit for staring into each other's soul. It was impossible. She was going bonkers.

Heather's voice broke the connection and Lily turned to her friend and began to breathe again.

"You don't need to ask," Heather said, "I'll tell you anyway. His name is Rick Anderson. He spent seven years in jail for vehicular manslaughter, and is serving a two year probation…"

"Wh…what happened?"

"He was driving drunk and killed an entire family… a mother, a father, and three small children. He was only eighteen at the time."

CHAPTER TWO

The Agony and the Ecstasy

Lily was still trying to recover from the twin assaults on her senses of the intense connection she had experienced, and of the revelation Heather had given her, when she felt a gentle tap on her shoulder.

Lily knew that turning to acknowledge the pressure would be crossing a line into pain, but she had no power to prevent it. Adjusting her position on her seat, she turned to find Rick Anderson's eyes once more staring into her own. There was no denying the torment she found there, but there was also something else, almost of recognition.

A conversation she had had with her father only a month before took only a second to flash upon her memory.

"Daddy, you have taught me to wait patiently for the man God has for me," She had squeezed his hand in a gesture that had become habit whenever seeking this godly man's advice, "but I'm twenty years old and I expected to at least have some indication from the Lord who he might be."

Angus Cameron returned the pressure of his daughter's hand, "You will know, Lily. You will recognize him. There will be no doubt at all." He paused, "There is, however something I must warn you of. Don't think the man God has for you will conform to some ideal you have built up in your imagination. God says in His Word,

'For my thoughts are not your thoughts,
neither are your ways my ways, saith the Lord.
For as the heavens are higher than the earth,
so are my ways higher than your ways,
and my thoughts than your thoughts.'"[1]

"What do you mean, Daddy? Am I not to have some expectations?"

"Sure you can, but be prepared for them to be adjusted as and when God reveals His will to you."

He grew silent for a moment, before continuing, "Lily, when God marks someone, either invisibly, or physically, as He has marked you, it invariably involves some period of testing designed to form that person's character according to His purpose.

"Jacob came away limping after wrestling with the Angel of the Lord. It marked, however, the end of Jacob's conniving ways. God marked Joseph for future usefulness, but he could not be used till he had been sold into Egypt, been falsely accused by Potiphar's wife, and spent time in prison.

"David was a fugitive in the wilderness for years before he was ready to take his place as king over Israel"

"Daddy, you're frightening me."

"There is no need for fear, Lily. 'There is no fear in love; but perfect love casts out fear, because fear involves punishment, and the one who fears is not perfected in love.' Whatever God calls you to go through it is because he loves you, and will turn out for your ultimate good."

"Must you always answer my questions with Scripture, Daddy?"

"I have nothing else to give you, Lily. Nothing else but what God declares in His Word."

The memory of that conversation had passed through Lily's brain faster than she could blink and continue to look into Rick Anderson eyes. The look of recognition was still there, as she was sure he could detect it in hers. They had never met before, yet it was as if their souls instinctively knew their destinies were linked.

"You're the one," Rick said in a voice that sounded strangled. "You *have* to be."

"Lily, I have to be going," Heather interjected, a frown of concern on her brow, "Will you be alright?" She gave a suspicious glance toward Rick, "Do you want me to stay?"

Lily barely heard her friend, waving a hand in a gesture that said, "I'll be fine. See you later."

Her attention shifted back to the man with the pale green eyes. She said, "You'll have to explain yourself." This time the sweep of her arm indicated Heather's recently vacated seat, "Please sit down."

Once seated, a not uncomfortable silence settled between them and each regarded the other like old friends meeting after an extended separation.

Lily felt she was existing in a bubble of unreality. How could she be thinking of this man as an old friend when she had never met him before in her entire life? Yet she felt as if she and he were like two sides of the same coin.

There was no mistaking the torment lurking behind his eyes; it was a torment she may have shared had her father not re-focused her attention from the blemish on her face, to the pursuit of inner beauty. And yet, inexplicably, she could not escape the conviction that their destinies were inextricably linked. Even more alarming, she instinctively knew that link would have its tragic and agonizing elements. Yet she could not withdraw from it; she felt like she had just met the purpose for which she was born. It felt weird, as if she was indulging in fantasy.

Heather would accuse her of being too much under the influence of her father, of believing the blemish on her face had some supernatural significance. Regardless, she could not ignore the certainty that this meeting with Richard Anderson was a kind of watershed; from this moment she would be compelled upon a path not of her own choosing. Whatever their lives had consisted of before was mere preparation for what was to come.

In spite of the instinctive awareness that she was headed into trouble such as she had never before imagined, she had to believe God's good purpose would ultimately be fulfilled in her life. She could not explain this to anyone, not even her father, but it was as certain as her knowledge that the sun would rise on the morrow, and the moon would shed its beams in the night sky. All these thoughts flashed through her brain at the speed of light, and when she glanced down at her hands they were trembling – uncontrollably.

"Are you alright?" Rick exclaimed, reaching over to still the shaking of her hands.

The jolt resulting from the physical contact passed through Lily's body like an electric charge, leaving her bewildered and uncertain how to proceed. The expression in Rick's eyes mirrored her own confusion, but when she withdrew her hands from his, their trembling had ceased. In its place was a calm that defied explanation.

Her next words to Rick were equally surprising, "So, Rick, what are we going to do about this?" Lily knew he was aware of what she was referring to; not only the first jolt of recognition but also the mutual attraction that was shocking in its intensity. She knew he had felt it, so there was no need to explain what she had meant.

His reply proved her instincts true, "I don't know. I was hoping our meeting would lead to some answers, but this is way beyond anything I imagined." His eyes still reflected the torment of a soul in despair, but now she saw something new there. Was it hope? Was it something more compelling and intimate than that? She shut that thought down. She could not allow her mind to explore that possibility. Not now. Perhaps not ever.

"Perhaps, Mr. Anderson..." she faltered. The formal address had been designed to create a distance between them – it had failed miserably. She tried again, "Rick... I was going to say we should do nothing. This is too bizarre. I only became aware of you twenty minutes ago, and we've only been talking for ten minutes. This happening between us is beyond weird. It can't be real. It would be better to ignore it – at least until we can put it into perspective."

"You felt it too." It was not a question. "I am sure your friend must have told you my history – the despicable and hateful thing I am guilty of?

"She told me."

"For seven years I lived in a state of torment, wishing it was I who had died, and not that sweet couple and their three little girls. Suicide occurred to me many times."

It seemed like a cold question to ask, but she was going to ask it anyway, if only to still the turmoil roiling within her, "What stopped you?"

He did not seem disturbed by her question, even to have expected it, though he did not immediately respond. When he did speak it was in measured tones as if uncertain she would believe him, "Believe it or not it is not that easy to commit suicide in prison. Apart from not having a rope or knife to carry it out, convincing myself it was my only option was not as hard as actually carrying it out. The will to live was so deeply ingrained in me it would have taken a superhuman effort to override it, or a level of despair I had not yet reached.

"I did come up with a plan that would relieve me of the responsibility of carrying out the deed myself, by getting someone else to do it for me."

"How would you do that?" Lily could hardly credit the direction this conversation was taking.

"In my view my part in killing that family was so despicable I was sure one or more of the inmates would be willing to exact revenge upon me. Even some of the rougher elements in prison would consider some crimes unforgivable and carry out some rough justice. I felt my crime fell into that category. Surely in the exercise yard with the inmates bunched together, someone could knife me and the guards would not be able to identify who had done it."

"How did you plan to bring that about?"

"I can assure you, even that option was not easy to contemplate. I decided I would start to describe in detail how evil my actions had been to provoke one or more of the inmates to take revenge. I even dropped hints that I would count it a kindness if someone would put an end to my misery."

Lily felt herself in a bubble of unreality as she said, "Obviously it did not work."

"No, it did not, and I'll tell you why." Rick paused, as if to gather courage. His breathing came in gentle gasps as he continued, "This is the part you may find difficult to believe. My words made absolutely no impact at all. I spoke the words but something, or someone, was preventing them from reaching whoever I was speaking to. They were completely unaware of what I was saying.

"That was the first time I began to suspect that something supernatural was going on, and that was when I began to pray."

At this point Lily felt her turmoil dissipate, and a peace she recognized as divine settled upon her. The inner voice she had heard before instructed her: *Do not be afraid. I am with you. Just move forward with this man. I will guide you both.* Lily did not doubt but that she was hearing the still small voice of God. She reached out tentatively and gently took hold of Rick's hands with both of hers. The jolt was milder this time, but just as real. She allowed her gaze to meet his. In doing so she felt his pain as if it were her own, and she knew she could not withdraw from this man. Their destinies were linked. She knew the path ahead would be rough, even laced with tragedy, but the certainty of God's Presence made the prospects more to be anticipated than avoided. She knew she was going to love this man. It was not love as yet, but the inevitability of it seemed certain. Their meeting was providential. They both had blemishes. Hers was on her face; his was on his soul. Somehow, she knew not in what manner, but God would use her own blemish to erase the blemish on his. It was too much to hope the reverse could also be true.

Sensing Rick was not done with his narrative, Lily squeezed Rick's hand to encourage him to continue.

"That night," Rick said, "I had a dream, or a vision, or whatever. In it I saw a man. I could not discern his features for the most intense light emanated from him. In the dream I was struck dumb and fell to my knees, certain I was in the presence of an angel.

"The voice emanating from this heavenly creature was otherworldly, echoing in deep tones of assurance: '*Richard Anderson. Your cries of distress have been heard, and after a period of anguish and distress you will find the peace you long for. Someone will be sent to aid you after your release from prison, a girl whose beauty has been diminished. Together you will walk a path through danger, heartache and hardship. Trust her. She is your link to the highway of holiness, and ultimate joy.*'

"I never had another dream like it, but the words spoken by the vision were indelibly burned into my memory so I can repeat them to you now. Lily, do you believe me?"

Lily withdrew her hands from his, but kept visual contact, "I believe you Rick, but I need time. I need to speak with my father. I cannot act without his advice, or prayer to adjust to this new reality. Let me know how to contact you and I will get back to you."

Rick had no doubt anticipated this for he reached into his pocket and drew out a paper serviette on which was inscribed his phone number.

Rising, Lily took the missive from his hand and turned to go, leaving him with one final word, "God go with you, Rick." And then she was gone.

Totally engaged in their own unusual encounter, Rick and Lily had been unaware their exchange had been witnessed by a man seated in the far corner of the coffee house. He had been too far away to hear their conversation, but had read their body language with such anger he could hardly contain himself.

Previously his ire had been directed at Rick Anderson, the man who had spent a mere seven years in prison for killing an entire family, including three little girls. In his view that was a mere slap on the wrist – a parody of justice. Since the justice system had failed, he knew it was up to him to balance the books; to even the score. Folks may call that vigilantism, but he called it righteous judgment; it was only right that Rick Anderson should suffer equal punishment for what he had done. The Bible said so – and eye for an eye. Since Rick's drunken driving had resulted in the death of his victims, only his own death would wipe the slate clean, and it was up to *him* to carry out that sentence.

The ante, however, had been raised. Lily Cameron had been stirred into the mix; she had joined herself with Rick Anderson. He had that kind of discernment. He knew instinctively their conversation had not just been a casual social encounter. Though he could not explain it, he knew they were now vitally connected. Their destinies were now inexorably linked.

Lily Cameron, despite the blemish on her face, had grown from a pretty girl into a beautiful woman. He had always admired her. It grieved him to realize that, having aligned herself with this killer of little children – this destroyer of families – she must suffer the same fate as Rick Anderson. Lily Cameron must also die.

The man sipped his coffee and remembered how he had entered this noble calling of what he thought of as "an angel of justice." He was convinced it was a divine mandate; God had chosen him to be an agent of destruction – an avenger of crimes against humanity, especially those who had no power to resist evil themselves. The little girls Rick Anderson had killed, and their parents, cried out for justice, and *he* was going to deliver it for them.

It had been a process that had led him to this phase of his life, but if he were to identify the moment it had become clear to him it was on a day three years ago when he had been reading the local newspaper. The report was a report of parents and other adults whom the police had arrested for sexual abuse on their children. In the end these had got off with a year in prison and a further sentence of community service, though their children had been removed from their care. In that moment he had known what God was calling him to. All seven of those abusers of children, including the parents themselves, had died in "accidents" by the following year. His brilliant mind had been able to devise these accidents and carry them out without even a whisper of suspicion arising from the police investigations. It was proof to him of the work to which he had been called.

And now God had revealed to him the next phase in his calling as an avenging angel. Rick Anderson and Lily Cameron had to die. It was just a matter of time and opportunity.

CHAPTER THREE

Adjustments

It had not taken two seconds after Lily had entered their home for Angus Cameron to know something significant had happened to her.

Even the blemish on Lily's right cheek had temporarily lost some of its red intensity. She looked as if she had had an intense white light shined in her face, giving her a startled look. She rushed to her bedroom almost unaware of Angus ensconced in his favourite chair, a book on his lap. His attempt to draw her attention was met with a short, "Not, now, Daddy," before she entered her room and gently, but firmly, closed the door.

Once ensconced in her room Lily sat on her bed and tried, by an act of the will, to stop the trembling of her body. Holding her flattened hand six inches from her eyes she willed it to stop shaking. She forced her breathing to slow, her lips uttering soundless prayers to regain control. It took several minutes before the trembling ceased and her breathing returned to normal.

She had been relatively calm when she had left the coffee house, but on the short drive home she had begun to feel like her brain was short-circuiting and her body was going into shock. She had had to make a super effort to concentrate on her driving, and once she had pulled into their driveway she had found the trembling of her body hindering her progress up the steps to the front door.

Now, once more breathing normally, she felt ready to engage in that discussion with her father she always had whenever facing a difficulty or trial.

Lily found him where she knew he would be, in his favourite chair under the intense lamplight directed over his shoulder onto whatever he was reading. His Bible lay open on the side table next to his chair, and the book on his knees, though open, was not attracting his attention. Lily saw the furrow of concern between his eyes as he lifted his gaze when she entered the room. It was not worry, exactly. Angus Cameron never worried. He lived by the rule laid down in 1Peter 5:6-7: *"Humble yourselves therefore under the mighty hand of God, that he may exalt you in due time: casting all your care upon him; for he careth for you."*

Asked once how he could carry the burdens of so many who came to him for counsel and not suffer burnout, he replied, "I never carry the burdens of others for longer than ten minutes; then I cast them on Jesus."

Nevertheless, Lily saw her father's concern was still within that ten minute range, and could possibly last longer. This was his "little girl" in the throes of some unusual crisis. She knew he would need more time to assess and process whatever was troubling her – and make it a matter of prayer.

Seeing her standing outside her bedroom door looking down on him, he said, "Come, Lily, "sit down and tell me what happened."

Lily took a straight-backed chair from the kitchen and positioned it directly facing her father. She sat in silence, but received no sign from him he was impatient for her to speak. He just regarded her with that mixture of indulgence and sympathetic regard he had always given her.

At last Lily met his gaze, "Daddy, do you remember when I was talking to you about the man God would choose for me to be with for the rest of my days?"

Angus gave her a nod of assent.

"Well, Daddy. I've just met him."

Except for the sound of traffic moving past their small house only silence met her declaration, her peripheral vision registered the tall blue Spruce tree through the open window. It loomed Christmas-tree-like, over the front porch, a landmark for anyone seeking to identify their house.

"You're sure?" Angus Cameron said at last.

"I'm sure Daddy."

"Tell me about it."

Though her body had stopped shaking. Lily's voice quivered as she recounted what had happened in the coffee shop, both before and after Heather had left her with Rick Anderson. She tried to convey, not only the details of what had happened, but also the emotional impact they had

had upon her. What impact they had had upon Rick she could only guess at, but she tried to convey her impressions to her father.

Lily had no words to describe the almost electric jolts that had passed through her as their hands made contact, or the sense of connection that was undeniable.

Nevertheless, by carefully placed questions her father seemed to have gained an accurate idea of the entire encounter.

Her eyes must have still conveyed something unresolved in their expression, for he asked, "What, Lily? What is still troubling you?"

"I'm scared, Daddy."

"What is scaring you, sweetheart?"

"It… it's something you told me some weeks ago. When I asked you how I was going to know the man God had chosen for me you told me that when God marks someone visibly or invisibly, it invariably means they would have to go through some time of testing."

Angus nodded.

"You cited Jacob, David and Joseph, all men who went through severe trials before realizing their potential."

Angus nodded again.

"Daddy, why would God choose a man for me who is so emotionally scarred? He is so damaged on the inside I am afraid I could not handle all that loving him will entail."

Angus rose from his chair and pulled Lily up and into his embrace, her head resting on his shoulder, "I don't know all the answers, Lily, but I believe God will give you the strength to bear it, and also to triumph."

"You see, Daddy, I feel like the blemish on *his* soul has somehow become mine. I feel his pain as if it were my own."

Angus released his daughter and held her at arm's length to get her full attention, "Perhaps that is the only way God can reach him and deliver him, Lily. Feeling his pain may be the one thing that will enable him to come out of it."

Richard Wadsworth Anderson had gained his middle name from his parents' love of the New England poet, Henry Wadsworth Longfellow.

Though his parents were nominal believers in the Bible, and in

Christianity in general, they had no personal experience of either. Instead, their love of literature and poetry acted as a substitute for personal religious devotion.

Of all the poets, the works of Henry Wadsworth Longfellow, and in particular his narrative poems captured their admiration and devotion. So, instead of growing up in a church environment and instruction in teachings from the Bible, Rick had been nurtured on the works of Longfellow, and others.

The fact that Longfellow's themes were distinctly Christian, either escaped his parent's notice entirely, or made such a vague impression on their minds as to make the knowledge inconsequential.

One narrative poem in particular stood out in Rick's memory and acted as a watershed, determining the direction his life would take. It was a poem entitled, *King Robert of Sicily*.

It was the story of King Robert of Sicily in ancient times who was incensed at certain words from the lips of Mary, the mother of Jesus. In her response to the angel's announcement that she would be the virgin mother of the Christ, she declared by prophetic inspiration:

He hath shewed strength with his arm; he hath scattered the proud in the imagination of their hearts.

He hath put down the mighty from their seats, and exalted them of low degree.

He hath filled the hungry with good things; and the rich he hath sent empty away.[2]

In Longfellow's poem, the king had defiantly declared, "No one will put me down from my seat."

It was a sentiment the eighteen year old Rick Anderson could fully identify with. He had nurtured in himself a sense of invulnerability. He was young, and he fully intended to carve out a future for himself on his own terms and nobody, just nobody, including God, was going to get in his way.

He hardly took notice of the rest of the poem chronicling the progressive humbling of the king.

Waking up in the church after making his proud challenge to the heavens, King Robert found himself in beggar's garb, filthy and clutching the chain attached to an ape, meant to assist him in the demeaning profession of begging.

Robert was totally incredulous at the position he found himself in. Taking it to be some cruel joke someone was playing on him he made his way to his palace gates, vowing dire consequences to the perpetrators. Arriving at the palace gates he was stopped by the palace guards. Making loud protestation that he was the king, and receiving incredulous and derisive response, he was eventually brought before the throne. With mingled shock and amazement Robert saw someone else seated upon it. The man sitting on the throne, wearing *his* crown and *his* kingly robes was no doubt an imposter, but to Robert's amazement he could have sworn it was he himself sitting there – the perfect image of himself. No one could have discerned any difference between them, except Robert was now dressed in the filthy garb and the imposter arrayed in kingly splendor.

Loudly protesting Robert declared, "*You* are an imposter, and *I* am the king!"

The angel sitting on the throne, for that is what he was, simply responded, "*You* are a beggar, and *I* am the king."

Thrust out from the presence of the angel, whom no-one recognized as such, Robert spent the following years in the humiliating role of a beggar. He slept on hay among cattle or sheep, his only companion the ape that helped him ply his trade.

From time to time the angel would appear to him with only one question for Robert, "Who are you, Robert?"

Still angry and defiant, Robert always answered, "*You* are an imposter, and *I* am the king!"

Gradually, however, after his anger cooled and his arrogance seemed to beat ineffectually against the hard wall of his circumstance, a change began to stir within him. The grandeur and incomparability of God settled undeniably upon his spirit, and his own unworthiness became increasingly apparent. At last he was sufficiently humbled for a longing to stir within him – a longing for change. From that moment on he waited patiently for the angel to come to him again.

When at last the angel came to visit him he was finally ready for the question the angel always posed.

"Robert," said the angel, "who are you?"

"*I* am a beggar," Robert replied, his eyes fixed on the ground at his feet, "and *you* are the king."

"No," said the angel, "*I* am an angel, and *you* are the king."

Immediately Robert found himself once more restored to his kingdom, arrayed in his own kingly robes. In the years that followed Robert became the most compassionate and just ruler his people had ever experienced.

During his seven years in prison, Rick Anderson had gradually begun to see the similarity between his own actions and that of King Robert. He, too, had been defiant. He, too, had felt in total control of his own destiny. He, too, had been humiliated. His time in prison was marked by, and burdened by, unbearable guilt for his part in wiping out an entire family. Rick Anderson knew his drunken driving had been inexcusable.

Like Robert of Sicily, Rick had had an encounter with an angel who had told him a girl with diminished beauty would ultimately lead him to a life of joy.

When he had seen Lily sitting with her friend in the coffeehouse with the blemish on her cheek he had known with absolute certainty *she* was the one the angel had spoken of. In his view, however, the angel had been wrong. The blemish on her cheek had not diminished her beauty; it enhanced it.

When his sister at last called him down to dinner he had not realized his encounter with Lily Cameron would be evident to others. As he took his seat at the table with Jeanie, her husband Josh, and their two children, Jeanie gave him an intense look, "What has happened to you Rickie?"

Rick met her gaze, "Why? What do you mean?"

"Something has happened to you." Turning to her husband, she asked, "Josh, is it just my imagination, but don't you see something different about Rick?"

"Not sure," Josh replied, clearly thinking his wife was acting oddly herself.

"I guess it must be a woman's intuition thing then. This morning when Rick went out there was a cloud of despair hanging over him. Now that cloud is gone and there's almost a spring to his step. Something has happened to him."

"Can we pray and start eating?" Josh replied. "You can figure it all out after dinner."

Rick sighed with relief when she acquiesced. He was not about to disclose anything concerning his close encounter with Lily Cameron anytime soon. Perhaps never.

Jeanie mumbled something under her breath before stretching out to grasp hands for the prayer of thanks.

"What was that you were mumbling under your breath, Jeanie?" Rick asked.

"Oh, nothing," Jeanie replied nonchalantly, but Rick thought he had heard her say, "Must be a girl,"

In the heavenlies two angels hovered over the small city of St, Catharines. Though they were situated near the stars, their supernatural vision allowed them to view the events on earth up close.

*The taller of the two angels, called **Magnificence**, addressed his companion, **Andromeda**, in soundless words, "The connection between the chosen one and the damaged one has been made. The graciousness of He-Who-Knows-All has been set in motion."*

Andromeda replied, "And what is our part in this? What are we to do with these frail objects of our Master's mercy?"

"Not all has yet been revealed to me," Magnificence replied, "but I can tell you this, the evil one has planned their destruction. He cannot afford to have the damaged one rise from the ashes of despair, or allow the chosen one to survive. Our role at present is to protect these two from the onslaughts of the Enemy, and block the attempts of the deceived one to destroy them."

"How are we to do that?" Andromeda enquired. "You know we cannot act on behalf of humans without the prayer required to defeat the enemy."

"I know it well," said Magnificence, "that is part of our assignment. We must stir the spirit of prayer in those surrounding our charges. But do not fear, we already have one who knows how to pray. We can start with him."

"Who is this praying one?"

"He is the father of the chosen one. The Spirit will stir him to such prayer as he has never known before. From his prayers an army of praying people will rise to defeat the devices of the enemy. All that prayer will enable us to act as we are directed."

"I have one more question," Andromeda said, "What about the deceived

one the Enemy is using to destroy our two charges. Will he be damned forever for his part in this human drama?"

"I do not know for sure," Magnificence replied, "but the Son of the Almighty is full of Grace. He has already paid for the worst of the sins of mankind. The deceived one is sincere in his belief God has called him to the role of avenging angel. If he can be awakened from the spirit of deception, there may be hope for him. At this point we cannot tell. All we can do is wait for this human drama to progress. At last, in the manner the Almighty has determined, all will be revealed."

CHAPTER FOUR

Developments

If Lily could be said to have a super power, it would be in the realm of church secretary-ship.

Perhaps she had been an answer to prayer, for the secretary who came before Lily in this mega church had followed the same standard of excellence Lily adhered to. To Lily, it felt like she had found her comfort zone – her natural environment in which she excelled without conscious effort. She had been told once that, if you loved what you were doing, you would not need to work a day in your life. And there was no question but that Lily loved what she was doing.

Yet today Lily was still reeling from her encounter with Rick Anderson, and something even more disturbing; she had a sense of danger that was almost palpable in its intensity.

It made no sense, for she was in the safest environment, both physically and spiritually, anyone could imagine. She was surrounded by godly men and women intent on serving God with singleness of heart and mind. Yet it was here, her spirit told her, that the danger lurked. Even if the danger did not emanate from one of her workmates, or from the pastoral staff, she felt certain it came from someone who visited these premises regularly. Perhaps there was even more than one.

In spite of none of this making any sense to her she could not shake the feeling. Knowing she could not perform her duties in a manner pleasing to God while this state of affairs persisted, she prayed silently: *Lord, help! I don't know what has come over me. Is this an attack of the enemy? Is the danger real, or is my imagination running away with me?* Almost before her prayer had ended, the answer came, settling on her spirit like oil on troubled waters: *The danger is real, but I will never leave you or forsake you.* Following that still small voice the sense of danger remained, but it receded into a deeper recess of her mind that did not unsettle her, or her ability to perform her duties. It was what it was and God would guide her through whatever was to come.

Thoughts of Rick Anderson, however were not so easily pushed into the background. All she could do would be to postpone dealing with them till her lunch-date with Heather. That best friend may not be able to still the mixed confusion and excitement that just thinking about Rick stirred within her, but she would at least provide a distraction.

The rest of the morning was occupied in answering the phone, photocopying, collating, and dealing with the numerous people who came to her with requests and conundrums to solve.

One of these was a pastor on staff responsible for pastoral counselling, Reginald Waters. He had the sweetest temperament of any she had ever encountered, besides her father that is. Lily had no doubt Reg was in the ministry tailor-made for him. A man in his early fifties, with almost thirty years missionary, pastoral, and counselling ministry, Lily could imagine the effect his warm gaze and sympathetic demeanor would have upon a troubled soul seeking his counsel. The thought even occurred to her she might herself seek his counsel in her present state of uncertainty, but something told her the time was not right.

"What can I do for you Pastor Waters?"

"Can you not dispense with the formality, Lily?"

"My father taught me to respect my elders, pastor, and it's a lesson I do not plan to unlearn." She delivered this with a winning smile that elicited an encouraging, "Admirable, Miss Lily. Truly admirable. But in answer to your question, yes, there is something you can do for me. I have some questionnaires that need to be typed and reproduced." He handed her the list of questions. They were clearly inscribed in his beautiful handwriting. A careful man, as well as a gracious one. "A hundred copies should do it. I hate to apply any pressure, but I need them this afternoon."

Consider it done, pastor. I can squeeze it in between printing out the weekly bulletin and the staff meeting before lunch."

"Thank you, Lily." So saying he turned and retreated to his office on the second floor. Seeing pastor Waters go, Lily reflected on how privileged she was to work amongst so many people who treated her with respect and were always so grateful for what she did for them. Heather certainly had to endure a lot more challenges in her workplace; disgruntled customers, demanding bosses, and unreasonable workmates. Not so her in this dream job. Even the frequent visitors from other churches seldom had any complaints. Even if they did, they expressed them in terms of quiet enquiry. Even the people making deliveries were seldom anything but respectful.

After printing out the weekly bulletin, Lily typed and printed pastor Water's questionnaires and carried them with her into the staff meeting, since pastor Waters would also be there.

As Lily entered the boardroom her sense of danger returned. It was not overwhelming, just an underlying feeling of unease. It caused her to take special notice of all those gathered, and she felt guilty for even thinking one of these good people could possibly present a danger to her.

There was the usual bustle and low murmur of conversation preceding the entrance of Jake Laramie, the lead pastor, and the official start of the meeting. This gave Lily time to cast her eye over those present, and to consider afresh her knowledge of each of them individually. In her wildest imaginings she could not believe *any* of them would be a source of danger – to her or anyone else. They were all godly people engaged both professionally and privately in the spreading of the Gospel, and in being a positive influence to the community at large. Perhaps the danger was not issuing from anyone in this room, but from some outsider passing by her desk on a regular basis. Pastors and members of other congregations, people seeking godly counsel, and people making deliveries were part of Lily's everyday encounters. Perhaps whatever danger threatened emanated from these, and not from her work colleagues she considered her friends.

Lily nevertheless began a review of those present. Her eyes first settled upon Samantha Williams, a mid-thirties dark-haired woman in charge of helping the needy from the church's benevolent fund. Again, she was a good fit for the position she held; compassionate and understanding of the sometimes tragic circumstances people found themselves in. Sometimes Lily detected something in her expression that hinted at some tragedy in her past that acted as a driving force for the compassion that flowed freely from her. No way could any malevolent threat emanate from her.

Beside Samantha sat a young man possessed of youthful zeal qualifying him for the position of *Director of Evangelism*. Kyle Stoddard wasn't really all that young, possibly approaching forty, but the energy radiating from him made him appear much younger. He reminded Lily of an athlete at the start of a race, eagerly awaiting starter gun to sound. He was ruggedly handsome, had a beautiful wife and two children reflecting their parents' good looks. She also crossed him off the list of a potential sources of danger.

Lily was about to pass her attention to the next one seated at the boardroom table when Pastor Laramie strode into the room and took his place at the head of the table, with a muttered apology for his lateness, "Last minute phone call," was his muttered explanation.

Pastor Jake Laramie was a man in his early sixties. He had a full head of brown hair, peppered with grey, with eyes alternating between grey and blue according to the mood of the moment. Lily was too far away from him to tell which colour predominated at the moment, but his warm interest in all gathered was evident. He had been leading this church as both founder and lead pastor for over forty years. These staff meetings were held so he could maintain a vital connection with each staff member, and they with each other. Any concerns could be freely expressed without fear of censure or criticism. No policy or monumental decisions were discussed in the staff meeting. Those were addressed by the ruling board. The staff meetings were for fellowship, support, and mutual encouragement.

By the time the meeting was over, Lily felt calmed by the positive tone the meeting had generated. Glancing at her watch she hurried to her desk, went to her handbag for her car-keys, and left for her lunch date with Heather.

"Are you totally out of your mind, Lily?" Heather ranted in an unaccustomed shrill voice. "You can't possibly be considering pursuing a relationship with Rick Anderson."

"I wouldn't call it 'pursuing" Heather, but I agree with you, my connection with Rick Anderson is certainly not conventional; it may even be termed 'shocking' in its intensity. But please try and understand, Heth,

I feel I have very little choice in the matter. I might even call it destiny, or a divine appointment. I have discussed it with my Dad, and he agrees with me."

Heather almost rolled her eyes. Lily was aware Heather believed she was very much under her father's thumb, but she had no confidence she could explain her relationship with her father in terms Heather would understand, so she kept silent.

"Have you seen the man since you met him in the coffee shop? Have you contacted him?"

"He has a name, Heth." Gently chiding her friend. Calling him "the man" was evidence of Heathers continued suspicion of his motives and intentions. "No, I have not contacted Rick yet."

"If you feel so strongly about this 'divine connection,' why not?"

"It's hard to explain."

"Try, Lily, but do it quickly, our lunch break is almost over."

"We could meet after work if you like, if you want a longer explanation, but I guess fear has something to do with it."

"Of what are you afraid?"

"I'm not sure exactly, but since my meeting with Rick I've had this inexplicable sense of danger. Even at work, which is the last place I should be feeling it. Somehow, moving forward with Rick has put me, and him, in mortal danger."

"Mortal danger? Isn't that a bit extreme, Lily? It's not like you to be so dramatic."

"Much of life *is* dramatic, Heth, at least spiritually speaking. Remember what the apostle Paul said about life's battles: 'For we do not wrestle against flesh and blood, but against the rulers, against the authorities, against the cosmic powers over this present darkness, against the spiritual forces of evil in the heavenly places.' (Ephesians 6:12 – ESV) But we'll have to speak about this later. We've both got to get back to work."

"After work, then. Same place, same time." So saying Heather rose and made her way to the door, but turned just before leaving, "I'll be praying for you, Lily. You can count on that." Then she was gone, leaving Lily with a strange sense of comfort at her friend's departing words. It was good to have a friend like Heather, in spite of her habit of expressing her sometimes blunt opinions.

Richard Wadsworth Anderson had no such comfort as Lily had gained from her meeting with Heather, 'Torment' would be a better word to describe what he was feeling. It was already Tuesday. After his connection with Lily on Saturday he had expected her to contact him. He had given her his phone number, but she had not responded in kind. So he was left with his emotions on edge, jumping in anticipation every time the phone rang, but the call had always been for another member of the household. Never for him. That was not exactly true. There had been one call for him from his parole officer, and another from *Social Services*. Those didn't count. His heart and his spirit cried out for a call from Lily Cameron, but she had not called.

Lily Cameron's failure to call impacted him from two diametrically opposed directions. The angel, or whoever the heavenly messenger he had encountered in his dream had been, had caused him to hope. He was sure Lily was the key to getting rid of the crushing load of guilt that plagued him. Ever since his drunken driving had caused the death of an entire family, including three little girls, guilt had been his ever present companion. The authorities thought his seven year's incarceration fit punishment for his crime; Rick felt nothing he suffered for the rest of his life would be sufficient payment for the deaths resulting from his irresponsible drinking and driving. He would gladly have spent an additional seven years in prison if he thought it would compensate for their deaths. He knew it never would. He could not explain the conviction on meeting Lily that she held the key to his emancipation – but Lily had not called.

The other direction Lily's failure to call impacted him, was the electrifying sparks; the thrill passing through him at her touch. He was certain she had felt it, too. He could not call it love. Not yet, but it had almost felt like a promise of things to come. It was accompanied at the same time by the knowledge he was damaged goods, and there could be no possible future for the two of them.

At this point in his deliberations there was a knock on his bedroom door. When he said, "Come in," his sister, Jeanie, swung the door open and took a step inside.

"Are you alright?" Jeanie asked, a wrinkle of concern appearing between her eyebrows. "You seem down-in-the mouth, though I did see a hopeful glint in your eye over the weekend."

"I'm fine," Rick said, unwilling to disclose too much about his state of mind, but grateful nevertheless for his sister's concern. She'd always been his loving "big sister," though before he had landed in prison he had thought her too nosey for her own, or his own, good. He knew now that "nosey" was not what she had been doing. Caring for him was a better description. She and Josh had taken him into their home without a murmur, and continued to make him feel welcome.

Rick knew he owed her a better response than what he had given her, so he raised his eyes to her concerned expression, "I guess I'm a little frustrated. My parole officer and Social Services have pretty much told me I won't get a job without their help. I'm going crazy sitting around waiting for them to contact me. And…"

"And what, Rick?"

He hesitated, "I've met a girl, sis. A beautiful girl, but it's hopeless."

A look of satisfaction passed over Jeanie's face, "I knew it!" She came in and sat beside him on the bed, "When you came home Saturday I could see a difference in you, I guessed it had to be a girl."

"A woman, Jeanie. She's a woman. I don't know why I referred to her as a girl. She's twenty years old."

"And she hasn't called you? You didn't get her number?"

"She didn't offer it, but I thought for sure she would call me. I know she's the one I was told about in my dream, but it's stupid to think about anything more than friendship happening between us. I know God means for her to help me, but anything more is just a pipe dream."

Jeanie rubbed his upper arm in sympathy, "She'll call, Ricky. I feel sure of it."

Lily and Heather sat at the same table they had occupied the Saturday before when the disturbing influence of Rick Anderson had entered her life.

In spite of it being Heather who was sitting opposite, Lily could not banish mental images of Rick's pale blue eyes, or of the thrill of his hands touching hers.

As arranged, she and Lily had met after work, with more leisure to discuss the concerns raised at their lunch meeting. What would she have done without this best of all best friends to share with, at least from an earthly perspective? Not to disparage the ever present support she received from her father, but sometimes a girl needed a girl's input, something Heather was always ready to provide.

Responding to the questioning expression on Heather's face, Lily said, "I think I've delayed contacting Rick because it's like landing on a foreign shore, with no guidebooks to ease my way. Apart from losing my mother at the age of ten, I've had a pretty smooth upbringing. My father's support and wise counsel has protected me from many of the knocks living in this world can deliver."

"That's not all it has protected you from," Heather said, an edge to her voice.

"Heather, I'm aware you think I've been too much under my father's thumb. But it hasn't been like that. His counsel may have left me unprepared for some of the challenges life may throw at me, but it has also given me spiritual resources I would not have otherwise developed."

With that I would have to agree," Heather said, with a smile of appreciation.

"On the other hand," Lily continued, "my decision to avoid dating and romance till God revealed who I was to marry has left me in a state of bewilderment now the man God has chosen for me has appeared. I feel like I'm alone in a boat far out at sea, with not even a glimpse of land to guide me."

"You actually believe," Heather gazed at her intently, "you have found the man God has chosen for you?"

"I think… no, I'm sure I have. He is just so far different from what I imagined he would be. I feel like I am teetering on the edge of a cliff and being compelled to jump."

"Lily, you're not seriously considering getting involved romantically with Rick Anderson. I know I've been urging you to start dating, but with Rick I see only trouble ahead for you?"

"So do I, Heth, but, and you're going to freak out at this… just his touch sent thrills of anticipation through me. Besides that I feel our meeting was a divine appointment."

With a look of resignation Heather said, "So, it seems there is nothing I can say that will dissuade you from involving yourself, either romantically or otherwise with this man?"

"With *Rick*, Heth. He has a name. But to answer your question, there is nothing you can say that will dissuade me. I can't escape the conviction God has brought us together for whatever purpose He has in mind. I'm afraid I'll just have to move forward, trusting the Lord to protect and guide us both. I would really appreciate your support, if not your agreement."

"Then, in spite of serious misgivings, Lily, you can rely on me not to badger you on the subject any longer. I'll support you whatever the future may bring."

"Thank you my friend. That means more to me than you'll ever know."

CHAPTER FIVE

Deliverance and Revelation

The two angels named Magnificence and Andromeda were again looking down on their two charges, the chosen one and the damaged one.

"The father of the chosen one has raised up enough prayer support for our next assignment, Magnificence said to his companion angel. We can act to deliver them from the fate the deceived one has planned for them."

"And what is that fate, great one?"

"Death, Andromeda. The deceived one is planning death for those we have been assigned to protect."

"The father of the chosen one must be a mighty prayer warrior to have gained such prayer support for such a vital assignment."

He is indeed, Andromeda. His prayers have caused the Almighty to stir the souls of a small army of praying people to pray for deliverance, even if those praying people Do not know for what deliverance they are praying for."

"The ways of the Almighty are beyond the comprehension of men," Andromeda replied, "and even beyond the understanding of angels. All praise to Him who sits on His Eternal Throne."

"And All Praise and Honour and Power for Ever and Ever to the Lamb of God Who was slain for the sins of all humanity," Magnificence added.

In the realm of nature there may well be what are termed *flawless* diamonds; diamonds that have no internal weakness that may cause them to break apart under pressure. In the realm of humanity, however, no such thing exists, something of which Lily was painfully aware.

The primary flaw in Lily's character could be described in one word – fear. More specifically she had a fear that love once given could be taken away without reference to the one to whom that love had been given. She knew this fear was rooted in her own experience, and that of her father.

Lily could not imagine a purer human love than that demonstrated by her father's love for her mother, yet her mother had been cruelly taken from him by the ravages of cancer. It had not been a sudden death, but one requiring him to watch, over an extended period of time, the fading of her beauty, and the pain he could neither relieve nor understand.

Lily knew Angus Cameron was fully reconciled to the loss of his great love, and to the manner of it. It reminded her of Job's declaration when he had lost his ten children and all that he had, "The LORD gave, and the Lord hath taken away; blessed be the name of the LORD."

Her father had been able to echo Job's heartfelt words. Lily had not. She could not understand his easy acceptance of it, though she recognized the depth of faith and devotion it must have taken for him to do so. Though she fought the idea with every part of her being, she saw her mother's death as an act of cruelty that could have been avoided. Could not God, who knew the depths of every human heart, have saved her father from the extended anguish of watching the love of his life die? He had not done so. Intellectually Lily knew there was reason and that reason was beyond her human understanding. Her heart, however, would not accept it no matter how many Bible verses she threw at it.

There was also her own personal pain to factor in to the equation. She had had time in the ten years she had known Madeline Cameron to experience the full extent of a mother's love. Only to have it wrenched from her in the cruelest manner possible. Her brain said, "There is a reason." Her heart said, "Love could not do such a thing." Therein lay the cause of her continued delay in calling Rick Anderson. If Rick was the love God had chosen for her, could He not just as easily snatch it away from her?

Lily had met Rick on Saturday and had been given his telephone number to call him. Given the double connection both of them had experienced, she knew he would expect her to call him. By Tuesday she had still not built up the courage to do so. Or Wednesday. Or Thursday.

Now it was Friday evening, and in spite of having to suppress the sense of danger at work all day, Lily knew she could not put off calling Rick any longer. Trembling slightly, she retrieved the serviette on which Rick had written his contact number, and dialed.

A woman answered, "Johnson Residence. Hallo."

Lily stammered, "Is… is Rick Anderson available."

"May I ask who is calling?"

"It's Lily. Lily Cameron."

"Oh, thank God, Rick's sister squealed into the phone, causing Lily to hold the receiver away from her ear. "Rick has been driving us all bonkers expecting a call from you. Every time the phone rings he runs down the stairs to ask who is calling."

The volume of Rick's sister's voice having returned to normal, Lily was able to return the receiver to her ear, "I'm Jeanie, by the way, Rick's sister. So glad to meet you, at least over the phone. I couldn't believe the spring in his steps when he came home Saturday after meeting you."

Lily could feel her cheeks turning pink with embarrassment at Jeanie's words. Rick's sister was certainly not the shy type, "Is Rick there?" Lily said, mainly to stop the flow of personal data coming from the other end of the line, "I would really like to speak with him."

"Oh, of course! Please forgive me. I was so excited for Rick's sake, I completely forgot to call him to the phone."

At least Rick had a loving family, Lily thought, even if his sister was a little overly boisterous. It may not be a good idea to talk too long on the phone with him. So when she heard Rick's relieved tone of voice, she merely said, "I think you will agree we have a lot to share with each other, and I'd prefer to do that face to face. Are you available to come for a drive?"

"Of course," Rick said.

"Give me your address and I'll come and pick you up."

Lily's next call was to Heather.

"And you're sure it's safe for you to go driving with him on your own. You know he's damaged goods, don't you?"

"That's precisely why I have to meet with him. Jesus ate with whole roomfuls of people who were damaged goods."

"OK, so you have to meet with him. Do you want me to come with you?"

"Heth, you promised to support me, even though you can't wrap your head around why I'm pursuing this relationship."

"So you are pursuing this relationship. You finally admit it."

"Yes, Heth. I *am* pursuing this relationship because I believe God is calling me to do so. Now, are you going to support me, or not?"

"OK, OK, I'll back off, but you can't stop me praying for you."

"I wouldn't expect anything less from you, Heather. Nothing at all."

Lily pulled up at the address in Port Weller where Rick lived with his sister's family. It was a two story dwelling with the same species of Blue Spruce in the front lawn as the one growing where she and her father lived.

The residential community on the south side of the Welland Canal had only existed since the early 1970's. Now, in 1980, it was only sparsely populated, though a number of houses were being built in the area. Many more were expected to follow. This was due to the dry docks and ship building facility located near the Welland Canal's Lock One. People working there would naturally wish to live nearby, as well as newcomers to St. Catharines.

From an upstairs window Lily saw Rick looking down on her and a few minutes later he came barreling out the front door to meet her. She breathed a sigh of relief, not being quite ready to meet Rick's family. In spite of the almost divine connection between the two of them the day they had met, Lily was only prepared to explore their relationship in tiny increments. Contemplating any more was more than her emotional equilibrium could at present sustain.

When Rick opened the passenger side door, took his seat, and turned excitedly toward her, Lily made a small movement away from him.

Recognizing that as a withdrawal, frown lines appeared between his brows, "You didn't feel the connection between us last Saturday? You didn't feel the almost electric thrill that passed between us, Lily Cameron?"

"I felt it," Lily said cautiously, "but you have to understand something Rick."

"Tell me."

"I have seen an example of real love between two people – the love between my father and my mother. I have seen it in a few other people and I have even felt a mother's unconditional love. In all those instances I have seen that love taken away, sometimes in the cruelest possible ways."

"That doesn't mean…"

"It doesn't mean that it *will* be taken from us if we learn to love each other. No, but in my experience it always *has* been taken away. I'm not sure I am ready for that. At least not yet."

Rick breathed a sigh of acceptance, "Okay, so where do we go from here?"

Lily took this as a double entendre and restarted her car, "We go somewhere private away from here to discuss this, and we take *baby steps* as we explore what the Lord may have for us in the future."

"Baby steps?"

"Slow and cautious."

"I don't feel that cautious."

"I do."

After a brief silence Rick asked. "Do you know where we're going for this discussion?"

Lily admitted, "No, but I thought you may have a suggestion."

"Turn right at the stop sign, and then left just before the bridge."

Following his instructions she found they were in a giant shipyard, with at least one ship in the process of building, and others being repaired. Being after hours it felt bleak and abandoned. Naked light bulbs gave weak illumination at the top of tall concrete poles. An almost full moon cast an eerie light over the facility, making the silhouetted buildings look like ruins. Lily shivered.

Sensing an unspoken question Rick said, "You said you wanted a quiet place away from my place."

"I… I didn't expect it to be quite so…"

"Isolated?"

"Away from any human presence."

"You're afraid to be alone with me."

"Not afraid, just not so… intimate."

"Well, let's get out of the car and walk. I promise I won't get even close enough to touch you."

Feeling somewhat reassured, Lily opened her door, exited, and started walking with him along the key side.

"You had a dream or a vision," Lily started off the discussion.

"I'm not sure which," Rick confirmed, "but I believe I saw an angel.

He told me someone would be sent to me who would help me relieve my guilt for the horrible deed I had done in causing the death of that family. The word 'horrible' was mine, not the angel's. I never thought I would ever be free from the guilt of what I had done. I still don't."

Lily stopped in her tracks, considering the account he had shared before. Had he really seen an angel in a vision? Somehow she could not doubt it. It was not a story a man like Rick would have made up, not if she considered the connections both of them had experienced. She had only one question, "What makes you think the angel was referring to me when he said a girl would be sent to you to help relieve your guilt?"

"He said she would be a girl whose *beauty has been diminished*. The blemish on your face was initially what made me believe you were the girl the angel referred to. The connection we both felt confirmed it. I still feel it."

Rick paused, "But let me tell you Lily, I don't believe the blemish on you face diminishes your beauty. I think it *enhances* it." The blush on her unblemished cheek reflected both embarrassment and pleasure at his words.

"I mean it Lily. I can see much deeper than the blemish. I see a girl who has pursued inner…"

He never got to finish the sentence. Rick never could explain afterwards what caused him to look up at that critical moment. Perhaps it was the grinding of machinery in his ears, or an instinctual sense of danger, but what he saw caused him to throw his arms around Lily, even knowing he could do no more than that before a crane dumped a load of steel rails upon them both. In the split second of comprehension he knew he would never be able to throw Lily out of the path of the deadly load. They were both going to die.

Incomprehensibly, the load of steel did *not* fall on them, but several yards away, though its crash on the concrete almost scared them half to death. In the aftermath of the crash, however, Lily found she was even more shocked by the realization of what having Ricks arms wrapped around her made her feel. Love didn't come this suddenly to anyone. Not in the real world. This had to be a divine intervention, a destiny she could not have escaped. She knew she could no longer take baby steps in her love for this man. She loved him as truly as if that love had grown over a long period of time. She knew instinctively he felt the same. It did not even matter to her if this love, of the same order of that between her parents, was taken from her. She would simply joy in this love as long as it lasted. At last she understood how her father could identify with Job's words, "The LORD has given, and the LORD has taken away. Blessed be the name of the LORD," and mean them. Lily knew now she could do the same.

Lily's thoughts, and the feel of Ricks body pressed so close to hers, was interrupted when he asked, "What just happened, Lily?"

"Wh… what do you mean?"

"Lily, I *saw* it. There is no way that load of rails was going to land where it did. By all the laws of science it should have fallen *on* us. One moment it was directly above us. I *knew* we were going to die. There was no time to get out of its path, yet it crashed down several yards away from us."

Lily, still trying to recover from the intensity of the feeling coursing through her as a result of Rick's intense embrace, asked him, "What do you *think* happened, Rick?"

Rick hesitated before saying, "I hardly dare to believe it may have been an angel?"

"Or two angels," Lily said, a sudden conviction taking hold of her. "I think the Lord must love you very much, Rick Anderson. He seems to be going to extreme lengths to preserve your life."

"And yours, too, Lily."

"And mine, too," Lily agreed, a deep gratitude to God overwhelmed her.

Suddenly aware they were still wrapped in each other's arms, they parted abruptly. Lily felt bereft, as if something precious had just been taken from her. Looking into Rick's eyes she knew he had felt it too. This was too much. In spite of knowing this was a divine connection she doubted her emotions could sustain such intensity, "You know we will have to go slow with this, don't you?" Lily said intensely. "It is all too much too soon."

Rick nodded, "I'm far too damaged for this, Lily. I'm afraid acknowledging what is happening between us will bring trouble on you, and I couldn't bear that."

"I know it will, Rick. I've known it from the very first. That is why I took so long to contact you. I knew we were headed into danger – and loss. None of that matters now. Our destinies have been joined, and denying it can only bring further pain. There is, however, one thing that must be dealt with before what is between us can reach fulfilment?"

"And what is that, Lily?"

"Your guilt, Rick, and the damage it has done to your soul."

Rick, was overwhelmed with two wonders. The first was that God may indeed love him in spite of the unforgivable act that had led to the death of an entire family. The second wonder was what he had felt when he had been holding Lily so close to him. He knew he loved her. It was undeniable.

That in itself was more than he could comprehend. Having only met her less than a week ago. What he felt for her went against every idea he had ever had of what falling in love would be like. The only possibility that made any sense was that their coming together was divinely orchestrated. He and Lily were meant for each other.

There were many challenges still to face, but love had crashed down upon them as suddenly as the iron rails almost had, blasting away any preconceived notions of what falling in love was expected to be. Gratitude welled up in him as never before, as well as the sense that it was altogether undeserved. He knew that, until the guilt that still clave to him could be removed, he could never fully embrace a future with Lily. While acknowledging the miracle of their deliverance from death, he was sure God would never forgive him. Even if, by some incomprehensible law of Heaven God *did* forgive him, he knew he could never, in a thousand years – forgive himself.

Humiliation

The man could not believe he had failed.

It had been a perfect set-up.

Following Lily to her assignation with Rick Anderson had taken patience, for he had expected her to meet with him long before this. Eventually, however, his patience had been rewarded. From a few hundred yards down the road he had watched Rick leave the house and join Lily Cameron in her car. When she drove away and he realized where they were headed, he exulted.

Before he had become a pastor he had worked in several shipyards. Operating cranes was his special ability. He felt sure the One who had called him to this work was arranging events to allow him to carry out the deed the justice system had failed to impose. A life for a life; in this case five innocent lives had been lost because of Rick Anderson's irresponsible actions.

Why then had he failed?

He had perfectly aligned the iron rails over the man and the girl. He was still a master of his former occupation, and there was *no* way the rails could have failed to crash down upon them.

Yet they had.

A split second before impact, the rails had inexplicably veered to the right and crashed harmlessly on the dock side, not even causing a scratch on the intended victims.

He had, of course, descended to ground level and made his escape, but not before he had glimpsed the two of them locked in an embrace that caused anger and frustration course through him. Love and fulfillment was not what ought to be in the future for these two. And he was going to make sure it never did.

Lily knew walking into Rick's sister's home holding his hand verged on foolhardy, but she no longer believed denying God's providential involvement in their relationship was the wisest course. The way ahead was anything but clear, but she knew she could not in any case be in control of the future. A verse in the book of Isaiah came to mind.

…fear not, for I am with you;
be not dismayed, for I am your God; I will strengthen you, I will help you,
I will uphold you with my righteous right hand.[3]

While Lily knew that promise was originally made to Israel. She also knew God was applying it to her present situation. She refused to descend into fear again. She would *trust and not be afraid*, another phrase from the book of Isaiah.

While Lily had expected an excited response from Rick's sister, based on their previous telephone conversation, she had not expected the squeal of delight that issued from Jeanie's lips. Or her arms wrapping around her in delighted welcome. Allowing her to see them holding hands may not have been the best idea ever.

At the same time the enthusiasm of Jeanie's welcome wrapped around her like a warm blanket. Letting go of Rick's hand, she returned the embrace.

Jeannie gave Lily an appreciative once over, "You're beautiful, and I can't tell you how pleased I am you and Rick are together. It's just what Rick has needed, after all he has been through."

"We… we're not exactly together…yet."

"Oh yes you are. I could feel it the moment you came inside, but I understand your hesitation. It must be all very new and sudden for you both." Her second perusal appeared not to even notice Lily's blemish. This seemed to be a family trait. She had had the distinct impression that Rick had seen *through* her blemish on their first meeting, and not *at* it. She had the same sense now.

Lily became aware of a rather good looking man standing in the background behind Jeanie, his dark brown hair displaying evidence of grey at his temples. On other side of him, a boy and a girl about ten and twelve stared at her with eyes the size of saucers.

"Oh, forgive my bad manners. This is my husband Josh, and our children Lynn and Jason." Lynn was blonde like her mother, and Jason seemed like a younger version of his father.

Josh came forward and shook her hand, "Glad to meet you, Lily." Though his demeanor stood in stark contrast to that of his wife, Lily could feel his unreserved acceptance of her. Lynn and Jason seemed too much in awe of her to give her much more than a mumbled, "Hallo."

Josh turned to his wife, "Jeanie, why are you making Lily and Rick stand in the entrance like this?" Turning back to Lily he said, "Please make yourself comfortable in the family room. Jeanie will get you some refreshments."

The rest of the evening would go down in Lily's memory as an update of what family life ought to be – imperfect people living in harmony despite facing many of life's challenges. Even in the hour Lily spent with them they shared some of those challenges. They were quite transparent about who they were. It came as no surprise to her that Rick's family had welcomed him into their home. It was clear they accepted how foolish his actions had been leading to the death of an entire family. They did not diminish his responsibility for the tragedy one iota. At the same time they did not allow that gross failure in his life to colour their appreciation of who he really was.

"We all need wake-up calls from time to time," Jeanie said. "What happened to Rick just happened to be a much louder wake-up call than most of us have to endure."

"Loud doesn't describe it," Rick said, an edge of bitterness in his voice. "More like a scream, if you ask me. I don't think I will ever be able to behold myself in the mirror without shame."

"Don't say that," his brother-in-law said, in a voice filled with regret.

"That's just the way I feel." Rick said, before recounting his experience with Longfellow's poem *King Robert of Sicily*, and how his arrogance had mirrored that of the king.

"Don't you see? I'm being punished for my arrogance. My arrogance was even worse than that of King Robert. He only suffered his own humiliation. Mine led to the slaughter of an innocent family."

Lily could tell Rick's family were familiar with the analogy, even the children, though she was hearing it for the first time. Not the poem itself. It had been a favorite of her father's, but the first time she had seen the intimate connection of it with the history of Rick's own humiliation.

"Don't forget how the poem ends, Rick," Jeanie pressed. "He was restored once again to his former glory, a changed man."

"I know, Jeanie, but it seems more like a fantasy to me, not something I can actually expect."

"Why not?" Lily questioned him. "Can't you see God's hand in all of this? Why don't you tell them about the miracle of deliverance you and I just experienced? Or shall I?"

To say Rick's family were shocked when he told them of their close encounter with death would be a gross understatement. He gave a blow by blow account of the iron rails coming down upon them, and their sudden inexplicable diversion to fall harmlessly on the concrete surface of the key.

"Don't *you* see?" Lily emphasized. "God delivered you because He loves you, and wants you to experience His forgiveness."

"I… I just assumed God saved *you* from death. My deliverance was only the result of me holding you in an attempt to get you out of its path."

"No!" Lily said with emphasis. He delivered us *both* because He is not finished with us yet. He has a special plan for your life, and for mine."

If God ever had a plan for my life, Lily, I screwed it up."

"You can't screw it up. Not if you're willing to accept what Christ has done for you." She turned to Jeanie and Josh, "Do you mind if I tell a story from the Bible, a story concerning one of the most arrogant men on the face of the earth at the time?"

"Please do," Jeanie and Josh said together, while Lynn and Jason nodded their heads enthusiastically. They appeared stunned by the adult talk so far, and were eager to hear more. Hearing that their uncle Rick and this new lady had been delivered from death must have sounded exciting in their youthful ears. Perhaps adult talk had bored them before, but not tonight. Their parents had forgotten to send them to bed, and they were about to hear another story.

Lily realized this family, in spite of their kind and accepting demeanor, were virtually ignorant of what was in the Bible. They seemed familiar with the poets, but as she had determined from what Rick had shared so far, were virtually strangers to the amazing truths contained in Scripture.

Aware she was speaking to children, and to adults who would be hearing things new to them, she shifted into the storytelling mode she adopted while teaching her Sunday school class. She dug into her handbag and retrieved a small Bible before launching into her narrative:

"There was a great king who lived around two thousand five hundred years ago. His name was Nebuchadnezzar, and he ruled over the entire known world at that time.

You can understand why he would have been a very proud man. He had what he saw as absolute power over all of the known world. Of course, God is the only One who has absolute power, but he did not know God, so he thought *he* had absolute power. He thought he had gained his great power by his own efforts, and that God had nothing to do with it.

"At this point in his life he had a dream from God. In the Bible Nebuchadnezzar tells his own story. She flipped through the pages of her Bible and read:

"'In the visions of my head as I lay in bed were these: I saw, and behold, a tree in the midst of the earth, and its height was great. The tree grew and became strong, and its top reached to heaven, and it was visible to the end of the whole earth. Its leaves were beautiful and its fruit abundant, and in it was food for all. The beasts of the field found shade under it, and the birds of the heavens lived in its branches, and all flesh was fed from it.

"'I saw in the visions of my head as I lay in bed, and behold, a watcher, a holy one, came down from heaven. He proclaimed aloud and said thus: 'Chop down the tree and lop off its branches, strip off its leaves and scatter its fruit. Let the beasts flee from under it and the birds from its branches. But leave the stump of its roots in the earth, bound with a band of iron and bronze, amid the tender grass of the field. Let him be wet with the dew of heaven. Let his portion be with the beasts in the grass of the earth. Let his mind be changed from a man's, and let a beast's mind be given to him; and let seven periods of time pass over him. The sentence is by the decree of the watchers, the decision by the word of the holy ones, to the end that the living may know that the Most High rules the kingdom of men and gives it to whom he will and sets over it the lowliest of men. This dream I, King Nebuchadnezzar, saw.' (Daniel 4:10-18 - ESV)

"After king Nebuchadnezzar had told his dream, Daniel gave the interpretation:

"'…this is the interpretation, O king: It is a decree of the Most High [God], which has come upon my lord the king, that you shall be driven from among men, and your dwelling shall be with the beasts of the field. You shall be made to eat grass like an ox, and you shall be wet with the dew of heaven, and seven periods of time shall pass over you, till you know that the Most High rules the kingdom of men and gives it to whom he will. And as it was commanded to leave the stump of the roots of the tree, your kingdom shall be confirmed for you from the time that you know that Heaven rules. Therefore, O king, let my counsel be acceptable to you: break off your sins by practicing righteousness, and your iniquities by showing mercy to the oppressed, that there may perhaps be a lengthening of your prosperity.'[4]

"Do you think the king took Daniel's advice? Not a chance. He was far too confident of his own power, and far too comfortable with his sinful lifestyle to take notice of what he probably thought of as 'a silly old dream.

"A whole year went by. He had no doubt forgotten all about the dream, but God had not forgotten.

"'At the end of twelve months he was walking on the roof of the royal palace of Babylon, and the king answered and said, "Is not this great Babylon, which I have built by my mighty power as a royal residence and for the glory of my majesty?" While the words were still in the king's mouth, there fell a voice from heaven, "O King Nebuchadnezzar, to you it is spoken: The kingdom has departed from you, and you shall be driven from among men, and your dwelling shall be with the beasts of the field. And you shall be made to eat grass like an ox, and seven periods of time shall pass over you, until you know that the Most High rules the kingdom of men and gives it to whom he will." immediately the word was fulfilled against Nebuchadnezzar. He was driven from among men and ate grass like an ox, and his body was wet with the dew of heaven till his hair grew as long as eagles' feathers, and his nails were like birds' claws.

'At the end of the days I, Nebuchadnezzar, lifted my eyes to heaven, and my reason returned to me, and I blessed the Most High, and praised and honored him who lives forever,

for his dominion is an everlasting dominion,
and his kingdom endures from generation to generation;
all the inhabitants of the earth are accounted as nothing,
and he does according to his will among the host of heaven
and among the inhabitants of the earth;
and none can stay his hand
or say to him, "What have you done?"

'At the same time my reason returned to me, and for the glory of my kingdom, my majesty and splendor returned to me. My counselors and my lords sought me, and I was established in my kingdom, and still more greatness was added to me. [37] Now I, Nebuchadnezzar, praise and extol and honor the King of heaven, for all his works are right and his ways are just; and those who walk in pride he is able to humble.' (Daniel 4:29-34 – ESV)

"Is that story really in the Bible?" Jeanie asked.

"It is," Lily replied, "and the reason I told it is because it closely parallels Rick's life. It also parallels Longfellow's poem about Robert of Sicily. Robert proudly declared no one would unseat him from his throne. Nebuchadnezzar proudly took credit for the power he had over the whole earth. And you, Rick, determined you were going to take control of your own life, and not let anyone, even God, have rule over you"

"So, what are you saying?"

"I'm saying that in every case God turned those proud declarations upside down. We don't know how long King Robert was humbled before he was humbled enough to be returned to his throne. In Nebuchadnezzar's case, he was humbled for seven periods of time, probably seven years. In your life, Rick, you also spent seven years in prison as a result of your proud declaration that no one was going to control your life."

"And what does that mean, Lily? Is God going to make me suffer some more for wiping out an entire family? Whatever punishment God demands from me will not be enough as far as I am concerned."

"No, Rick. You are missing the point. Once Nebuchadnezzar's reason returned to him, he was restored. I believe the time of your humiliation is *over*. God means to restore you, forgive you, and cause you to become one of His children."

"How in the world is He going to do that, Lily?"

"I'll explain how, Rick – and to anyone else who wants to listen."

CHAPTER SEVEN

Uncertain Days

"So why haven't you gone to the police?" Heather fired the question at Lily after she told her of their near dramatic escape from certain death.

"What are we going to tell the police? They will just tell us it was an accident and we were fortunate no one was injured. Indeed, it may have been an accident. We did not see or hear anyone there. The place was deserted except for the two of us."

"And Rick Anderson wrapped his arms around you?"

"Only in an attempt to save me from almost certain death."

"Which didn't happen. How do you know Rick didn't plan it ahead of time, just to get close to you?"

"Heather, you are really being quite ridiculous. You seem quite determined to dislike Rick. Sure, his drunk driving led to disaster, but he paid for that in jail for seven years, and isn't he just the kind of person Jesus wants to save. He was criticized for eating with tax collector's and sinners."

Heather looked suitably ashamed, "I'm sorry Lil, and it's just that I don't want you to get hurt, either from physical danger or from a broken heart. I promise to treat Rick with grace and kindness in the future."

"You'll have a chance to follow through on that promise, Heth. Rick is meeting us here in about fifteen minutes. I'll expect you to show him every kindness and consideration. There is, however, one shocking reality you will have to get used to. I'm still in shock myself, but it's true."

"What is true, Lily?"

I love him Heth. I can't explain it, and I know the path ahead will not be easy. It doesn't make sense, but I love him."

"Lily! You *can't* love him. You only met him a week ago."

"I know, but do you think love follows a time table? It will take time to work out that love in real life situations, but the reality of it cannot be denied. I'm not ready to say those three little words to him yet, or allow him to say them to me. I *do* love him.

"I know, however, that love that comes this suddenly has to be worked out in real life. Just because we are meant for each other doesn't mean it will not present challenges. In fact, it may be even more challenging than the love that grows at a more leisurely pace. With Rick's inner struggles, it could be even more so."

"What about Rick's responsibility for the death of that family? Heather said, a stubborn edge of prejudice still in her tone.

"God will forgive him, Heth. I know He will."

"Does *he* know he can be forgiven, Lily?"

"Not yet, but I believe the process has begun. In any case I think the problem now is not so much whether or not God can forgive him. I believe it is more a matter of whether he can forgive *himself.*"

"What did you mean when you said you thought the process has begun?"

Lily took a deep breath, "I'll have to tell you quickly, Heth. Rick is due to arrive any moment. I saw it last night. After I told the story of Nebuchadnezzar, his humiliation and restoration, I saw the light of understanding dawn on his face. The process has begun, Heather. I'm sure of it."

At this point in their conversation Lily became aware Heather was staring at her. While that was understandable considering the discussion they had been having, Lily sensed there was more to it than that.

"What? Why are you staring at me?"

"Lily why are you wearing makeup?" Heather asked. "You have never worn makeup before. It's a point of conviction with you. You are not ashamed of the birthmark on your face and you've never seen the need to hide it."

"I'm *not* wearing makeup, Heather. I have never worn it before and I see no sense in starting now."

"Why then has the blemish on your cheek faded?"

Lily dug into her handbag and retrieved a mirror. Staring into it she almost gasped in wonder. The birthmark on her cheek was distinctly paler than she had ever seen it before.

When Rick Anderson arrived at the coffee house he was out of breath.

He had elected to run down the trail beside the canal instead of taking the bus. Besides having limited funds for bus fare he found walking gave him more time to reflect on Lily's visit the night before. The miraculous deliverance from certain death was impossible to put down to coincidence. In that split second of awareness he had seen the rails coming straight down on top of them. Without a miracle there was no way they would have survived. Perhaps Lily had a point and God did have a plan for his life. In spite of his unforgivable involvement in the death of innocents, God seemed to be protecting him, though he had assumed the deliverance had come because of Lily, and not because of him. His deliverance had merely been a side benefit of Lily's deliverance, which she deserved and he did not.

And then there was the story Lily had told she said was from the Bible. He could not deny how similar the pride and humiliation of that ancient king was to his own life experience. Longfellow's poem of *King Robert of Sicily* was also a close parallel. Did that mean God intended to restore him as well as He had those two kings?

Once he left the canal trail he had to navigate Welland Avenue to the coffee house. Being a little late for the agreed time for their meeting, he ran most of the way up from the canal.

Once at the entrance to the coffee house he took a minute to catch his breath before entering. He cast his eye over the patrons before locating Lily and her friend in the far corner to the left. He felt nervous at the prospect of spending time with Heather. He had met her only briefly the previous Saturday. Even in that short time he had sensed her disapproval. He guessed her suspicion of him stemmed from her protectiveness for her best friend. After all, he had just come out of prison and would still be on parole for a further two years. In her mind he must represent a threat to Lily's safety and future happiness.

Apparently, though, Lily had been speaking to her, for she seemed to make a special effort to be friendly. She greeted him pleasantly as he took his seat beside Lily who gave him a welcoming smile. He reached for her hand under the table and wondered how he would ever get used to the jolt of electricity that passed through him whenever their hands met. Even considering the reality of the connection between them, Rick knew Lily was setting limits upon the progress of their relationship. Holding hands was as far as she was willing to go. He understood this. Their romantic connection had been sudden and irresistible, but getting to know each other on a deeper level would take time. These things could not be rushed.

Turning his attention back to Heather, Rick knew the challenge she represented had to be faced head on. In spite of her pleasant demeanor there was an edge to it he sensed rather than observed.

"Heather," he said levelly, "may I call you Heather?"

"Of course. That is my name."

"Because Lily is your best friend it is pretty certain we will be together on a regular basis. I just want to be sure there will be no tension between us."

"That would be good," Heather said noncommittedly."

"Tell me if I am wrong, but you seem to think Lily and me pursuing a relationship is not a good idea. You think what I did was unforgivable and seven years in prison does not wipe the slate clean."

"I have felt that way. You are quite correct."

"Alright, so here is the thing. I agree with you."

Heather's lips set in a straight line, "Then why are you holding Lily's hand under the table?"

Rick met her stare with equal intensity, "With her full consent, Heather." He felt Lily squeeze his hand in confirmation, making his heart soar higher than the clouds. She must have given Heather a nod of affirmation, for her friend's expression softened.

"So explain to me, Richard Wadsworth Anderson, how you can agree with me that you and Lily hooking up is not good for her, and yet you persist in pursuing her?" The use of his full name spoke volumes. She had researched him. Her love for her best friend burned with a protective zeal that would not permit her to back down before all her concerns had been laid to rest.

"I don't know, Heather. All I can say is that our destinies seemed to be linked. Neither of us can find fulfilment apart. After Lily shared the story of Nebuchadnezzar from the Bible a hope was born in me that God intends to restore me, whatever that might mean. Longfellow's poem about

King Robert of Sicily seems to convey the same message. Both of those men were humiliated as I have been – for seven years. It is beyond my understanding that God would be willing to do so, but Lily has convinced me He intends to do so."

"So you are bold enough to assume you are in love with Lily after only having known her for barely a week?"

"I will not say those three little words to her, though I cannot deny they are true. My love for her may be a fact, but I will not expect the fulfilment of that love till the guilt and condemnation that still possess me has been removed. At present I can hardly imagine that to be a possibility."

Lily spoke up, "Heth, this is not as sudden as you may think. You, as a believer, know that God works in mysterious ways. Let Rick share with you the dream – or vision – he had at the lowest point of his despair in prison."

Her interest peeked, Heather nodded, "So tell me."

So Rick recounted his experience with the heavenly visitor, giving every detail as he remembered it. He saw Heather's expression soften by degrees as the narrative unfolded. When he moved from the account of the heavenly visitor to the miraculous deliverance on the Port Weller docks, he saw the last wall of her resistance crumble.

"I tell you Heather, there was no way those rails could have missed us. I was looking up at them coming directly down upon us. Lily had made it clear there should be no touching, but I threw my arms around her to throw her clear. There just wasn't time to do that. I *knew* we were both going to die. The rails were no more than ten feet above us when we heard them crash down at least fifty feet away. It was then I began to believe in miracles. In the aftermath we were both trembling in shock and neither of us felt the need to separate. In spite of only meeting less than a week before, we *knew* we belonged together."

"Apart from beginning to believe in miracles," Heather enquired, "was there anything else that happened. Before you and Lily parted?"

"I told you about that," Lily interjected."

"I want to hear it from Rick, Lily."

Rick drew in a long breath before answering, "When Lily told the story of that king from the Bible, how his pride caused his humiliation for seven years, I saw how closely my story compared to his."

"And what effect did that story have upon you, Rick?"

52

After a moment of silence, he said, "For the first time in seven years, I felt hope."

Rick was surprised when Heather laid a comforting hand on his arm, "That is a marvelous beginning, Rick. I am sorry I have been so judgmental. Put it down to the protectiveness, or, if you like, overprotectiveness. I feel for my best friend, but I want you to notice something."

"What is that?"

"Look at the blemish on Lily's cheek."

He turned his gaze upon Lily beside him but all he could see was her left cheek, free from any blemish at all, till Lily turned her right cheek toward him."

"What do you want me to see, Heather?"

Rick, when I saw her blemish this morning I thought she was wearing makeup, which she never does. When she assured me she had not applied any makeup at all, and told me about your response to the story of Nebuchadnezzar, I realized something. The blemish on Lily's cheek has faded. Not a lot, but it has definitely faded. And then I had another thought. The fading of her blemish began when you began to understand that restoration was possible for you ...when you began to have hope."

Turning her gaze upon Lily, Heather said, "Do you think it is possible that this connection between you and Rick is so vital that when Rick's inner blemish is relieved, the blemish on your cheek lightens?

"At this stage," Lily replied. "I can believe almost anything."

The man found the disguise he was wearing somewhat uncomfortable, but he had found it necessary in order to hear the exchange between the three young people in the next booth. He could not risk Lily recognizing him.

It had been initially acceptable to observe them from the other side of the coffee house, but after his failed attempt on their lives the night before he had to probe for the reason behind his failure. Hearing their conversation could give him valuable insight as to what had happened. If Lily saw him this close she may just make the connection between his proximity and the events of the night before. It was not likely she would, but he could not afford for anything to go wrong.

The adhesive on the white beard, moustache, and eyebrows itched.

The pads on the inside of his cheeks were designed to alter the appearance of his face so the chance of recognition was diminished. The wig, beard, and pads reduced that possibility to near zero, but it was uncomfortable. He considered the discomfort well worth the information he could gather.

The man bristled at what he was hearing. He could not accept that the rails had been diverted from their course by angels. God would not permit it, since God had called him as an administrator of justice when the justice system failed. There had to be another explanation. The failure was nevertheless inexplicable. It created a sense of unease within him.

The anger in him rose to boiling point when Lily's friend mentioned she and the killer were holding hands under the table. Clearly the connection between these two was increasing. The idea that Rick Anderson could be experiencing the joys of romance caused his anger to meld with a dangerous level of frustration. Together the two emotions created a pressure cooker effect within him that, if not released, could explode. If that happened he could not imagine what the consequences would be.

All the man in the elaborate disguise knew was that he had to make plans to eliminate these two, and possibly Lily's best friend as well. He had sensed that young lady's hostility toward Rick Anderson had almost completely drained away, which made her complicit in the crime the Anderson boy had committed. They would *all* have to die.

CHAPTER EIGHT

Conflict in the Heavenlies

After Lily had dropped Rick off at his sister's home she pulled away from the curb and found a parking area adjacent to a nearby business. The events in her life were moving at such a pace she felt like she had been sucked up by a tornado and was being whirled around at a speed that had her brain reeling.

If it had just been a speeding up of the ordinary day to day activities she felt sure she could have handled them without too much trouble. There was nothing ordinary about what had been happening to her in the past week. Without marking them off on her fingers she ticked them off in her memory.

First, there had been her meeting with Rick. If the undeniable connection with him had not been startling enough, fast on its heels came the thrill of their first physical contact. It had been like an electrical charge passing through her entire body; a thrill so unexpected she simultaneously recoiled from it and longed for its continuance.

Waiting for God to reveal to her who her life mate was to be she had absolutely no experience with a close relationship with a man. Other than her father she did not know other men. She had not even met her male cousins, who live in the States. The young men she met at church were just acquaintances. She was on friendly terms with everyone she encountered at work, but her only real friend was Heather. When it came to forming close encounters with the opposite gender, she was in alien territory.

Then there had been the miraculous deliverance from death she and

Rick had experienced, resulting in that close embrace she had wished would never end.

There was no doubt in Lily's mind but that supernatural forces were arrayed against them, as well as angelic beings assigned to protect them. Being the centre of such supernatural conflict was amazing, but nothing else could have precipitated such a dramatic deliverance. A verse from Paul's letter to Ephesians came to mind: *For we do not wrestle against flesh and blood, but against the rulers, against the authorities, against the cosmic powers over this present darkness, against the spiritual forces of evil in the heavenly places.*[5]

A battle must be raging in the heavenlies focused on two insignificant individuals, Lily Cameron and Rick Anderson. Divine providence was doubtless at work in both their lives. It was past wonderful, and extremely humbling.

Lily's meeting with Rick's family also impressed her with two wonders; their sweet spirits, and their total ignorance of Scripture. They hardly seemed to know the church existed. Her reading of Nebuchadnezzar's humiliation and restoration had had a stunning effect upon them, and the first glimmer of spiritual understanding had appeared on Rick's face.

Thinking of faces, not one of them seemed to even notice her blemish, that led to another shocking reality: the blemish on her cheek had faded. Was there really such a connection between her and Rick that, as the truth began to dawn upon Rick, so the blemish of her face began to fade also? It hardly seemed possible. Did God really work that way? Or was He simply making them understand the correlation between inner and outward beauty?

Finally, there was the sense of danger that accosted her at work, and lingered in diminishing intensity as she got further away from her work environment. Except today at the coffeehouse. She had felt the danger lurking only feet away from where she, Rick, and Heather, had been sitting. She had turned, but all she had seen was a white-haired older man placidly sipping on his coffee and taking a bite from an apple fritter. There was no way the danger could have emanated from him – yet she had never felt the danger so near, or so maliciously directed at her.

When Lily arrived home she had barely had time to put her key into the front door when she heard the most agonized groaning coming from the front room. She had heard her father engaged in earnest prayer before, but detected a new level of anguish in his voice that alarmed her. She turned the key in the lock and entered, making her way to her room. It was her standard practice never to interrupt when her father was praying, but before she was half way to her room he called out to her, "Lily! We need to talk."

She turned to find him still on his knees, but facing her. His cheeks were wet with tears, lines of anguish marked his face.

"What is the matter, Daddy? I've never seen you quite so troubled before." Going to him she sank to her knees and gripped his hands in her own.

"Lily, you are in great danger."

"I know I am Daddy, and so is Rick. I have been feeling it for days now. But how do you know?"

Angus eased himself back onto his chair, drawing Lily closer, "How do you think I know Lily?"

"Has the Lord laid a burden of prayer upon your spirit?"

"He has, and more so than ever before. Lily, I am afraid for you... and for this man the Lord has brought into your life. Our Lord must have some great plan for the two of you, for the enemy seems to be wanting to shut down my intercession. I have never had such darkness hover over me as when I seek to intercede for you and your young man."

Lily silently tried to absorb what her father was telling her, and a quiver of fear passed through her.

At last she said, "Daddy, I have to tell you what happened last night. You were sleeping when I came home, and I heard you praying in your room when I left to meet with Heather and Rick today I didn't want to disturb you. But you are right. Rick and I are in great danger."

Lily then told him how someone had used a crane at the Port Weller docks to try and kill them.

"Rick saw the steel rails diverted only feet before they would have crashed down upon us. I think angels were sent to deliver us.

"And that is not all, Daddy. For the past week I have felt an undeniable sense of danger at, of all places, where I work. Surrounded by all those godly people seeking to serve the Lord, and those who visit us from other churches, I feel I am in mortal danger. I prayed about it and the Lord has kept it from overwhelming me, but it always seems to be looming in the background. I am never wholly free from it."

"This sense of danger?" Angus asked, "Do you ever feel it away from your workplace?"

"Nothing but a vague sense of it. Except this morning."

"What happened this morning, Lily?"

"Heather, Rick and I were drinking coffee and discussing Heather's suspicion of Rick's motives. The danger assaulted me so strongly I had to look to see where it was coming from. In the booth next to ours was a white haired man with a beard who sat drinking his coffee, and placidly munching a doughnut. I couldn't imagine the danger coming from him."

"Is there anything else you want to tell me, Lily?"

Lily took a breath and could not keep the tremor of excitement from her voice when she said, "Yes, there is, but I can hardly convince myself it is really happening."

"What is happening?"

Instead of replying directly, Lily turned her head so her father could get a good look at her right cheek.

He stared at it intently before saying, "Your blemish has begun to fade. When did you first notice it?"

"Heather pointed it out to me this morning. She thought I had begun to apply makeup, but it had definitely faded. I think it must have begun last night when I was visiting Rick's family."

"What happened during the visit that could possibly explain what is happening to your blemish? It has always been a rather intense shade of red. Now it is definitely not as dark as it has been."

"I was reading to them from the book of Daniel about Nebuchadnezzar's humiliation and restoration. I thought I saw a flash of comprehension come over Rick. I think *my* blemish began to fade when *he* began to believe."

Magnificence said to Andromeda, "I think we are going to need reinforcements."

They were both looking down at the dark cloud gathering over the town of St. Catharines, only discernible to angelic eyes. The cloud was more thickly concentrated over two places below; one over the residence of Lily Cameron and her father, and the other over where Rick Anderson lived with his sister's family.

"The demons are gathering," Andromeda replied." They are going to fight to gain control over our charges. Will we have enough reinforcements to prevail against them?

Only as many as the prayers of the faithful can gain for us. As one of their own has written, "Nothing is accomplished in Heaven or earth, except by prayer."

"And do we have sufficient prayer for us to prevail?"

Magnificence pointed, and immediately the inside of the Cameron residence became visible. The bent form of the chosen one's father could be seen, his body trembling from the intensity of his praying.

"The question is, can he sustain this intensity for much longer? He has hardly eaten for days now."

Andromeda called to mind what had happened to the prophet Daniel, recorded in the book bearing his name. He was in a similar position. In his own words:

"And behold, one in the likeness of the children of man touched my lips. Then I opened my mouth and spoke. I said to him who stood before me, "O my lord, by reason of the vision pains have come upon me, and I retain no strength. How can my lord's servant talk with my lord? For now no strength remains in me, and no breath is left in me.

"Again one having the appearance of a man touched me and strengthened me. And he said, "O man greatly loved, fear not, peace be with you; be strong and of good courage." And as he spoke to me, I was strengthened and said, "Let my lord speak, for you have strengthened me."

(Daniel 10:16-19 – ESV)

"The Almighty," Magnificence declared, "and His Son, has allowed us to do the same for this man, and for the chosen one, as the angel did for Daniel. She is weeping tears of intercession for the damaged one, though her strength is at a very low ebb now.

"She looks so frail," Andromeda said. "She hardly looks strong enough to bear the trials that still lay before her."

"And so we must touch her, too, with a strength beyond her own.

Andromeda. Come, let us do for them both what the Almighty and His Son has commanded."

When Lily arrived at work on Tuesday morning the sense of danger she felt around her had increased tenfold, but so also had her awareness of God's Presence.

She had marked a passage in her Bible the night before, and in the few moments before work began she took out her Bible and read it again:

...fear not, for I am with you;
be not dismayed, for I am your God;
I will strengthen you, I will help you,
I will uphold you with my righteous right hand.
Behold, all who are incensed against you
shall be put to shame and confounded;
those who strive against you
shall be as nothing and shall perish.
You shall seek those who contend with you,
but you shall not find them; those who war against you
shall be as nothing at all.
For I, the Lord your God,
hold your right hand;
it is I who say to you, "Fear not,
I am the one who helps you."[6]

Lily knew those words had been spoken to ancient Israel, but she felt they had special significance for her as well. They seemed to fit her case, and the challenges that lay before her.

She also knew her faith in those words would be tested to the nth degree.

Her mind went back to Saturday when she had been kneeling by her bed, close to despair with longing and fear for a man she now knew she loved. She had only known him for a week, but the connection between them was undeniable. Their destinies were inextricably joined, but the awareness of it had exhausted her. Her strength of mind and body had diminished to dangerous levels. Seeing her father in such agonizing prayer had made her afraid of what was to come – a fear she could neither deny nor overcome.

And then, at the very lowest level of her weakness, strength had begun to flow into her. Her body and mind were renewed. Hope sprang up unbidden from the soil of despair, and she rose up from her knees ready to face whatever was to come. She found her father, too, had experienced the same surge of unbidden empowerment, and she knew that supernatural forces were at work.

Lily had to put her ruminations aside when Andrew Wheller, the pastor of a nearby church addressed her, "Hallo Lily, do you think Pastor Jake could squeeze me into his busy schedule without a formal appointment? I have something important to discuss with him."

"I'll ask him, pastor." So saying she connected with Pastor Jake, listened briefly, then turned back to Pastor Andrew, "He said if you could wait for ten minutes he'll fit you in." He took a seat, and while she busied herself with various tasks she managed to give Andrew Wheller some attention without seeming to stare.

He was a man in his mid-forties, with a reputation for fire and brimstone preaching. Apparently his congregation appreciated him, because no matter how direct his preaching was, it was said he delivered it with genuine concern for those under his care. He always closed his messages with a call to commitment to the cause of Christ. By all accounts his people loved him, and his church was experiencing a spurt of growth.

Only since the sense of danger had come upon her had Lily begun to take a closer look at those who passed her desk, as well as those she worked with on a daily basis. She mentally crossed Pastor Wheller off the list of those posing a threat. He was far too genuine in his love for the truth, and in the care of his flock.

After a busy morning she chose to take her lunch break in the sanctuary rather than in the kitchen with her fellow staff members. She would go without food and spend the time thinking about the radical new direction her life was headed in. Some people longed for adventure, but A thrill of fear passed through her as she contemplated what the future might hold. She remembered what a writer of Western fiction had said about adventure: "Adventure is just another word for trouble, and anyone over twenty who goes looking for it is a fool." Or words to that affect.

Without warning a sudden stab of fear assaulted her. Instead of diminishing it intensified. It grew and joined the growing sense of danger to form a malevolent spear of aggression… Before long she felt it probing into her back like a living thing. It settled in at the base of her skull and she cried out. *Help me, Lord!*

The prayer had hardly left her lips when a Bible verse invaded her mind, as if it had been thrust there as the answer to her need: *Submit yourselves therefore to God. Resist the devil, and he will flee from you. Draw near to God, and he will draw near to you.*[7]

Lily fell to her knees. *I submit to you, Lord. Help me to resist this demonic intrusion into my life.*

Immediately the fear and the danger left her, cast out, she was sure, by a mighty hand. She was shaking in the aftermath of the attack, but she rose and turned to confront whatever and whoever had been assaulting her. A shadow moved at the edge of her vision, a mere silhouette in the shape of a man. It disappeared before she could focus upon it.

Somebody was out to get her. She knew it instinctively. She was just as certain Rick was included in the malevolence that had been aimed at her. She prayed for his protection and deliverance. She knew instinctively this was only the *beginning* of the trouble that lay before her and Rick Anderson. Alone, she knew neither of them were equal to what lay ahead, but they were not alone. Part of a Bible verse came to her, almost like a voice in her brain: *"I will never leave you nor forsake you."*

Lily knew Rick did not have the understanding to resist an attack like she had just experienced, so she fell to her knees and cried out to her Lord for his protection.

Chapter Nine

Questions and Answers

Rick did not have the spiritual resources Lily had when the malevolent assault came upon him. Only a glimmer of understanding of what Lily had been telling him had penetrated the guilt possessing him for the past seven years.

He had no way to fight the hate he felt was directed toward him. The cry of fear and despair that came from him was more like a scream. It brought Jeanie pounding up the stairs. She burst into his room and found him curled up on the bed in the fetal position. When he turned to look at her his eyes showed stark terror. Knowing not what else to do Jeanie wrapped her arms around him, holding him close. "What is it brother? What is the matter with you?"

The answer came out like a whimper, "I… I don't know."

Whether it was Jeanie's loving embrace that restored him, or something else, Rick could not, at the time, tell. Later he learned it had been Lily's prayer. He had not known she had been praying, or that she had experienced the same spiritual assault he had. The difference was his own ignorance of what was happening to him, robbing him of the ability to fight it. He was in awe when Lily told him later she had had to battle on his behalf.

"Hardly had the calm returned when the phone rang. Jeanie and Josh had arranged for an extension to be installed in his room so he would not have to rush down the stairs to answer the phone. He snatched it up.

"Hallo,"

"Rick, its Lily. Are you all right?" The concern in her voice was palpable.

"Why? Why would you think I might not be?" He had not meant his query to sound so short and demanding.

There was silence on the other end of the line before she asked, "Did something bad just happen to you?"

How did you know, Lily?"

"Because it happened to me, and God showed me how to resist it. Because of our connection I was sure I wasn't the only target. The enemy doesn't want us to be together, Rick. God has a reason for creating this connection between us."

"Lily, you are not making a lot of sense."

"I know. It's a lot to take in if you've never been exposed to God's truth like I have. May I come over after work? I'll try to explain it to you. At least, some of it."

"Just a minute." He turned to see Jeanie, her ears almost twitching with curiosity. "May Lily come for a visit tonight?"

"Of course. Tell her to come in time for supper. I have a few questions to ask her myself. More than a few. Josh and the kids as well."

Rick placed the receiver back to his ear again, "Lily, Jeanie would like for you to come for supper. We usually eat around six. We all have a lot of questions."

I'll do my best to answer them. Rick, I have to get back to work. Just keep trusting that the days of your humiliation will soon be over."

"I'll try, Lily."

When he heard the click at the other end of the line he replaced the receiver in its cradle.

"What was that all about?

"I'm not altogether sure, Jeannie. Something about the enemy assaulting us and learning how to resist him. We'll have to wait to hear more."

Jeannie came over and gave him a hug, "Rick, you know we all love you. Right? None of us in this family hold anything against you for what happened. It was a terrible tragedy when that family died. You may have been responsible for their deaths, but you didn't do it deliberately."

"I know that, Jeanie, but if I hadn't been so stubborn and irresponsible they would not have died. And I'm not worried about other people blaming me, Jeanie. I am perfectly capable of doing that – all by myself."

"But you *paid* for that, Rick. Seven years in prison is no mean payment."

"That doesn't bring that family back to life. It won't wipe the guilt for what I did from my soul, if I even *have* one."

Concern lined Jeanie's brow, "Don't give up hope, Rick. Lily seems to believe that guilt can be removed." She paused, "There is something beautiful about that girl that has nothing to do with how she looks on the outside."

"Do you think I don't know that, Jeanie? I just don't think I'll ever be worthy of her."

Lily felt like a celebrity when she walked through the Johnson's front door and was ushered into the kitchen, which was large enough to double as a dining room.

Everyone present had their eyes fixed upon her, as if they expected her to perform a miracle, or solve life's riddles with a snap of her fingers. She knew her first task would be to deflect attention from herself. She would have to refocus their attention upon God and His plan for their lives. *Show me how to do that, dear Lord.* On the heels of that silent prayer came a well-rehearsed verse she had always tried to live by: *Not by might, nor by power, but by my Spirit, says the Lord of hosts.*[8]

Now she knew what she had to do.

Stopping abruptly on her way to the dinner table Lily saw the startled look on all their faces. Knowing she had their attention, she said, "I know you're expecting me to answer all your questions, but I have to tell you I don't have any answers for you."

The startled look never left their faces, "B...but..." Josh stammered, "We thought that is why you came over tonight. To answer our questions. Ever since you told us the story of that king from the Bible the other night we have wanted to know more. Even the children."

"And after what happened to Rick this morning and you told him it was an attack from an enemy, we have been confused," Jeanie added. "You said you wanted to come over to answer our questions."

"Perhaps we should sit down and I'll explain."

"Of course," Jeanie said. She brought the roast to the table, and when they were all seated Lily asked, "Would you mind if I asked a blessing for the meal?"

"Why… no. Please go ahead."

After she had prayed over the meal, Lily said, "When I said I did not have any answers to your questions I did not mean there are *no* answers. I just meant that *I* don't have the answers you are looking for, but God has. After we have eaten I will try to answer your questions from the Bible. God inspired the writers of the Bible to write down His thoughts, and His plan for our lives, but let us first enjoy this wonderful meal."

It was a silent meal, each one occupied with his or her own thoughts. Even Jason and Lynn, as young as they were, seemed distracted, as if they were wrestling with the fundamental issues of life. Lily had no doubt but that the Holy Spirit was preparing all the hearts of those around the table for the ultimate presentation of the Gospel message. Having had virtually no contact with the Bible or church, a wonder in itself, a slow buildup of foundational Biblical truth was essential. It was up to her to provide it.

After they were all settled in the sitting room, Lily turned to Rick, "I have good news for you, Rick."

"And what would that be, Lily?"

"You have already fulfilled the first requirement for gaining forgiveness from God, and ultimately your restoration. And the one thing you most want to get rid of is the best thing that could have happened to you."

"I don't understand. What could that be?"

"Your *guilt* for what you did to cause the death of that family."

"You can't be serious, Lily. Guilt is the very *worst* thing that has happened to me."

"Only if you hold on to it, Rick. And only if there isn't a way to remove it. So let me ask you a question. Do you ever want to go back to the way you were living when you got drunk and caused the accident?"

"Absolutely not. I was a fool to think I could control my own destiny. Look where it got me."

"So, you have *changed you mind* about how you were living then? You have had a radical change of attitude from when you were eighteen?"

"Yes"

"In other words you repented. That is what it means to repent. To change your mind about the way you want to live; to change your attitude.

And repentance is one of the things God demands of you if He is to forgive you. So you have already met one of the requirements for God to forgive you."

"I suppose I have. I don't ever want to be proud like that king in the Bible, or like the king in Longfellow's poem."

So, tell me Rick, what was it that caused you to change your mind about the way you were living? What caused you to repent?"

"I'm not sure,"

"Wasn't it the *guilt* you felt for what you had done? The guilt you felt then, and the guilt you feel now was what led you to repentance. Without the guilt you may never have repented, and never been able to be forgiven for what you have done. So guilt was one of the best things that could have happened to you. Guilt is what God has designed our conscience to do to protect us from following the wrong path. When we feel guilty we know we need to change the direction our lives have been going in. Guilt is what makes us know we need forgiveness and God *has* made a way for us to *be* forgiven. If we felt no guilt we would feel no need to seek God's forgiveness, and find eternal life."

Rick looked only half convinced, "So what if I don't *deserve* His forgiveness?

Lily glanced around at the other members of Rick's family before she answered. She wanted them to understand this as much as she wanted Rick to understand, "That's the thing, Rick. *No one* deserves to be forgiven. We all owe a debt none of us can pay for. God's forgiveness and salvation is a *gift* none of us deserve. You don't have to deserve it to receive it."

Rick shook his head, "That can't be right, Lily. Bad deeds have to be paid for. Forgiveness cannot be dished out like some cheap trinket bought at a dollar store. Especially not for something as bad as I have done. *Somebody* has to suffer for the wrongs perpetrated against innocent people."

Lily rose from her seat and went to take Rick's hands in hers, "That is just the thing, Rick. *Somebody* already has suffered for what you have done – and for the rest of us, too."

The man sat in his study and considered his friend over his large oak desk, then shifted his gaze to the bookshelves covering three walls of the room. The

shelves were filled almost to capacity with books collected over a period of more than twenty years.

They were books of theology, philosophy, and history, both secular and religious. Except for a few on the bottom shelf he had read them all; he had meditated upon them, absorbed them, forming in the process the life principles by which he now lived.

His friend seemed to be in no hurry to find out the reason for his summons to this private conference, which suited the man admirably. He wanted to reassess the man's suitability for the task he wanted him to participate in.

He was a man of considerable talent, even looking the part of an artist with long hair, scraggy beard and clothing reminiscent of the 1960's hippie movement. His friend had a wide range of artistic capabilities, not least of which was in the realm of photography. What qualified him most for the task, however was his total agreement with his own pursuit of justice. When the justice system failed he was ready and willing to punish the unpunished and to bring down vengeance upon those who abused innocent victims. Indeed, he had done so on several occasions. He and his friend were a perfect match.

His silent assessment over, he addressed him in conspiratorial tones, "You know I failed to destroy Rick Anderson and his girlfriend, Lily?"

A nod was his friend's only response. He seemed to be waiting for the full picture to emerge.

"I plan to make another attempt in a month or two... after careful planning. My last attempt seemed providential and its failure inexplicable, but it has opened up another possibility.

"And what may that be?"

"To destroy the girl's reputation, and to cover them both with aura of shame. I plan to kill Lily Cameron's reputation before finally killing her, Rick Anderson, and her loyal friend."

"And you want my help? How?"

"By using your skills in photo manipulation. I've seen some of your work in that regard. I want you to create images that depict Lily in shameful situations."

"You know creating images like that is not a perfect science. Experts will be able to detect they have been manipulated?"

"No matter. It will take time for the images to be examined and proved fraudulent. By that time the damage will have been done. It is like breaking

open a pillow full of down feathers and letting them fly away in gusts of wind. It is virtually impossible to gather those feathers together again. Rumours will fly like those feathers, and there will always be people who will believe them, no matter how much proof is presented that they are unfounded. That is the legacy I want to leave Lily Cameron for aligning herself with that man. That legacy will last long after the day I kill them."

The passion of the man as he delivered, what amounted to a rant, pervaded the atmosphere of the room, causing his friend to nod in agreement.

"I would love to do what you ask for free, my friend, since this is such a noble cause, but in the interest of a starving artist I will have to demand a fee."

The man knew starvation was the least of his friend's concerns, but he replied, "Not a problem. How much?"

Once the amount was mentioned and agreed to the artist said, "I will need pictures of the subjects."

"You're the photographer. You will have to get those yourself."

"Give me a week or two and I'll give you what you want."

"It's been a pleasure, as always, to do business with you."

"Thank me once your goal has been realized."

"That I will, my friend. That I will."

"What do you mean?" Rick asked, "*Who* has suffered for the death of that family? I know I spent seven years in prison for vehicular manslaughter, but it has never seemed to be enough to pay for such a terrible deed."

"It is certainly not enough. Not if *you* were required to pay for it yourself, Rick. But God does not *expect* you to pay for it yourself. He knows you could never suffer enough to cover the sins you have committed, even without that one despicable deed. None of us can for any of our sins. So God took care of it *Himself*.

"I think I'm beginning to understand, "Jeanie interjected, "Somebody suffered in your place."

"Not just in Rick's place, Jeanie, but in yours and mine, and in the place of every sinner who has ever sinned."

"What do you mean by sin?" Josh asked.

It was a question that led to many more, from the adults as well as from Jason and Lynn, who were sent to bed long before the questioning ended.

It was after midnight before they were all too weary to ask any more questions, or for Lily to answer them.

Rick saw her out the front door, but as they stood on the steps outside under the porch light, Lily gave Rick a searching look. He looked different somehow, in a way she could not quite identify.

"What is it, Rick?"

"What do you mean?"

"You look different, as if a light bulb has suddenly come on in your brain."

"I didn't know it was that obvious, but yes, something is different. I *feel* different. All that you shared tonight started to make sense. About Christ suffering for my sins, and about angels, the devil and demons; about Heaven and Hell and things to come. I think I am beginning to believe. Perhaps there *is* hope for me after all."

At that point he gave her his own searching look.

"What? Why are you staring at me like that?"

To her surprise he gently framed her head with his hands and turned it so he could get an unhindered view of her right cheek under the porch light. His touch sent something course right through her that was at once disturbing and thrilling; something she wanted to repel, yet never wanted to end. She knew she should not permit such liberties, but could not pull away.

"Lily, I am not the only one who looks different tonight. When you get home, take a long look in the mirror at your right cheek. The blemish, if you want to call it that, has faded even more than it has before. Am I going crazy, Lily Cameron, or am I looking at a miracle?"

CHAPTER TEN

Discussions and Conversations

"It seems to me," Heather said to her two friends as they walked together along the trail beside the *Welland Canal*, "that you two ought to be spending more time together."

It was amazing to Heather that she now classified Rick Anderson as "friend." Her suspicions, and to be honest, antagonism, had been understandable, but, she now acknowledged, unfounded. Openly confronting the tension between them, and admitting he was not good enough for Lily, had won her over.

Added to that was his account of an angelic visitor while he was in prison. It was too fantastical a story to have been made up. If he had made it up he would have realized it was too fantastical to be believed, and toned it down to make it more acceptable.

He had done nothing of the sort. He had described the event with total sincerity, and included the detail of the "girl" having diminished beauty. He had added that he did not consider Lily's beauty to have been diminished by her blemish, but enhanced, which fell in line with Heather's own view. There were also a number of events that pointed to supernatural involvement in their coming together. The attempt on their lives at the Port Weller docks and their miraculous deliverance was one; the fading of Lily's blemish was another.

Heather glanced at the blemish, still distinguishable on Lily's cheek, but considerably less so. The connection between Rick's growing understanding of God's truth and the fading of Lily's blemish, was too evident to be denied. And Rick's sincerity was as evident as the smell of a rose is to the one breathing it in. Damaged and laden with guilt he might be, but he was genuine to the core. Yes, she could call Rick Anderson her friend.

She was brought out of her reverie by Lily's response to her declaration that she and Rick needed to spend more time together. She had not responded immediately, but seemed to have given it some thought, "Perhaps you are right, Heth, but somewhat impractical at present. With work responsibilities we will have to fit any quality time in between my other duties."

"I think you need more than that," Heather said. "I think you should take a couple of weeks off work and cement your relationship by spending some quality time together. After all, this sudden connection between you, and your emotional attachment was too sudden to have any depth. You need uninterrupted time to cement your relationship."

"She's making a lot of sense, Lily." Rick said."

"But what about my work? I can't be away too long or things will pile up."

"What do you do when you take your annual leave?" Heather asked.

"Carolyn Wendell, the former secretary stands in for me. She does even a better job than I do."

"Well, then. You have your solution. Go to Pastor Jake and request some time off. I am sure Carolyn would be amenable to the idea. She may be retired, but she will appreciate getting back into it for a while. She loved it before. She'll love doing it again for a couple of weeks."

"You're very convincing, Heth."

"As every good friend ought to be. There are a number of neat places you could go, *Balls Falls*, and *Morningstar Mill* for a start. You could go on picnics, drives to Hamilton, visit Niagara Falls, and take a ride on *Maid of the Mist*."

"I think you may have convinced me, Heth."

"Good. Maybe I'll go down in history, not exactly as the one who brought you two together, but the one who helped to deepen your relationship."

"You'd deserve every accolade I can give you, Heather," Rick said sincerely. "It seems I'm going to be in your debt."

"And don't you forget it, *Mister* Anderson," giving him a satisfied smile. It was far better to have Heather working *with* him than *against* him.

When Lily arrived at work on Tuesday she had a plan; she would continue her search for the source of the danger surrounding her, and meet with Pastor Jake to request personal leave.

The potential source of danger she would pursue by assessing the visitors who came to her desk, and at the staff meeting after lunch. She still could not conceive of the danger emanating from anyone she worked with or even from those visiting from other churches. Those unconnected with the church, who were either delivery persons, people coming for counsel, or having appointments, were equally unlikely sources of the danger.

That the danger existed she had no doubt. It was palpable, like a living thing, and her experience in the church at lunchtime last Friday proved to her how malevolent that danger was. The man she had seen in silhouette confirmed her belief the danger emanated from an individual under demonic influence. Without divine aid there was no way they would not crumble under the forces of darkness arrayed against them. The promise, however was sure: *"I will never leave you nor forsake you."*

Lily remembered a well-known preacher on the radio explaining that verse in depth. He said the word "never" in the original Greek had five negatives attached to it, so it was not just saying *"I will never leave you nor forsake you."* It was saying, "I will never, no never, no never, no never, no never, leave you nor forsake you. That message had been incredibly comforting to Lily at the time, but even more so now.

She reflected that she believed God when he said something once. If he said it twice, she would believe it even more firmly. But when God said the same thing *five times* in one statement, her faith in that statement would be *immovable*.

In remembering that insight courage not her own flowed into her. She and Rick *would* prevail against the enemy.

Lily was not prepared for the reaction of people to the fading of the blemish on her face. It was now only a shadow of its former intensity. People who had grown so accustomed to seeing her blemish they hardly noticed it, were suddenly confronted with how little they saw of it now.

It was as much a shock to them as if seeing the original blemish for the first time.

Pastor Jake was the first to notice the fading of her blemish as he passed her desk on his way to his office, "Lily, have you been going for special treatments?"

"No, pastor. I think the Lord is doing it. I'm not sure why."

The variety of responses to the fading of her blemish was somewhat amusing. Or not.

Jocelyn in Prayer Ministries asked, "Have you been praying for its removal, Lily?"

"No, Joss. I have never even thought of doing so. I have always thought of my blemish as God marking me for His purpose." The strange look Jocelyn gave her indicated what a foreign idea Lily's perspective was to her.

A frequent visitor named Wilma Parks, whose daughter had been crippled by a debilitating disease, asked bitterly, "Why would God heal the blemish on your face, and leave my Cindy in the state she is in?"

The only reply Lilly could giver was, "I don't know, Wilma. I really don't know."

Samantha Williams, administrator of the benefit fund, simply said, in her usually compassionate voice, "I am so glad for you, Lily. This healing could not have happened to a nicer person." Causing Lily to blush.

Arnold Sorenson, director of Group Life Ministries, was a man in his fifties who had given up his own church to develop cell groups. He believed large churches were prone to becoming disconnected to the individual; they lost intimate fellowship with other believers.

"Lily, I never thought the mark on your cheek was really a blemish, though you must be relieved it is fading"

Lily scratched him off her list of the potential source of the danger,

So it was the entire morning. Staff, visitors, delivery persons, and those keeping appointments all reacted to her fading blemish in different ways. All passed her scrutiny as being unlikely to be the source of danger. Before lunch she was able to use the time to assess a few members of staff before Pastor Laramie arrived to lead the staff meeting. The Director of Youth Ministries also passed her scrutiny. In his early thirties, Joshua Maine had a friendly demeanor that drew youth toward him, and the aura of a leader that inspired them to follow him. Andrea Simons was

Administrative Assistant to Pastor Jake, a position she carried out with the utmost efficiency and dedication. Lily crossed Andrea off her list, as well.

After the meeting was over and everyone dispersed to perform their various duties, Lily drew Pastor Jake's attention, "Pastor, may I have a private interview with you?"

When at last she was seated across from him in his office, Lily made her request for special leave.

"So you want some away time from your job, Lily. Are you finding it stressful? I would not have thought that of you. You are a perfect fit for the job."

"No pastor, I am not stressed." She was not about to mention the sense of danger surrounding her here. "I just need some personal time to pursue some personal goals."

Pastor Jake gave her a perceptive look, "Would this personal time have something to do with romance?"

Lily blushed, but could not prevaricate, "It *could* have something to do with that, pastor."

"Now don't be embarrassed, Lily. I have always wondered why you refuse to date any of the young men you come into contact in this church. I suspect, however, that you have been waiting for God to reveal to you who your life mate is to be."

"That is correct, pastor."

"And have you met him, Lily?"

"I believe that I have."

Pastor Jake drew in a breath, "And are you going to tell me who this fortunate individual is"

"His name is Rick Anderson, pastor."

An alarmed expression spread over the pastor's face, "Not the Rick Anderson, the one responsible for the death of that family; the one who has just been released from prison?"

"Yes, pastor. He is the one."

"Lily, you *can't* be serious."

"I am afraid that I am, pastor. He is the one God has chosen for me."

Pastor Jake stood and came around his desk to address Lily directly, "Lily, I am going to grant your request for special leave, but not for you to pursue this relationship. Rather, I want you to use the time to give more serious thought regarding it."

"I won't change my mind, Pastor. Rick is the man God has chosen to be my life mate."

"Lily, don't be stubborn. A man like that can get you into some serious trouble."

"I already know that. God has shown me the path ahead is going to be full of trouble, but that it will ultimately work out for *our* good, and for *His* glory."

"That is good theology, Lily, but have you considered you may be wrong and you are simply making a mistake?"

"May I go now, pastor? I have much work to do before Carolyn can relieve me."

"Yes, Lily, you may go, but not without my having a great deal of fear and trepidation for your future. I will be praying for you both."

Lili kept her own counsel when she returned to work. It had been necessary to reveal to Pastor Jake who the Lord had chosen for her, and she was certain he would not share his knowledge with anyone else. It was part of his code of conduct as a preacher and a man of God. He would not disclose confidential information without the person's express permission to do so.

His reaction to what she had shared, however, had convinced her it would be unwise for her to be silent about it for long. Heather knew, and she was on their side. Beyond that, it could not be hidden, nor did she want it hidden. She was not ashamed of what God was doing in their lives, but for now she would not spread the news abroad. She would put it all in God's capable hands.

Lily had no wish to deny her romantic feelings for Rick. Love had finally come to her, and in spite of the challenges, she wanted to shout it from the housetops. For now, though, she felt a cautionary nudge not to share this with her colleagues quite yet.

Lily found encouragement at home, but especially in her frequent visits with Rick and his family. Her father, as always, was supportive. Visits with Rick and his family were marked by endless questions. Lily sought to answer those question by endlessly referring to Scripture. She had gifted them all with Bibles in a translation easy to understand. They all sat in the living room, Bibles open, questions pouring out of them like a tap that could not be shut off.

One of the questions directed at Lily was one she delighted to answer. It came from Jeanie, who seemed particularly eager for answers.

"You say there is nothing we can do to save ourselves. There is nothing we can do to earn God's forgiveness. How then can we buy in to what Christ did for us on the cross, when He died in our place? It is clear to me people are not automatically forgiven because Jesus paid the price of sin. You have made that point more than once, but there must be a way to apply what Jesus did to our own lives, *personally.*

"That is correct, Jeanie. Jesus dying for us is a *provision*. Soap and water is a provision so we can cleanse our bodies. If we do not apply soap and water to our bodies, they will remain dirty. If we do not apply what Jesus did for us on the cross, we can never be clean from our sin.

"So your question is how can we apply what Jesus did for us on the cross to our lives personally?"

"Yes."

"I have the answer for you, Jeanie, but first I have to qualify the *nothing* you referred to earlier. There is nothing you or I can do to *merit* the salvation Christ provided for us by His death and resurrection. The good works we do cannot save us because they are simply *not enough*. God is not asking us to just *stop* sinning if we are to earn our own salvation. The requirement is that we must *never ever have sinned* to be worthy of Heaven. That is impossible. *All* of us have sinned and fall short of the glory of God."

"Then how can we be sure of Heaven if there is nothing we can do to earn it?"

"Remember, Jeanie, I said there is nothing of *merit* we can do to *earn* salvation. It is a gift. Turn to the book of Romans chapter six, and read verse twenty three." By this time none of them had much difficulty turning to the right book and chapter. Lily read the verse while the others followed in their Bibles. *For the wages of sin is death, but the free gift of God is eternal life in Christ Jesus our Lord. (Romans 6:23 – ESV)*

"There are only two things you can do with a gift, *accept* it, or *reject* it. If you accept a gift you cannot pay anything for it, or it is no longer a gift. So yes, there is *something* you must do to receive eternal life. You must *accept* it as a gift, not as something you have worked for.

"So now I have to ask," Rick said, "How does someone *accept* this gift?"

"Rick, I can give you the short answer, but the answer is so important I'm going to give you the long answer. I have told you about the two robbers who were crucified with Jesus. Let me read to you what Matthew says about them." Turning to the passage, she read:

So also the chief priests, with the scribes and elders, mocked him, saying, "He saved others; he cannot save himself. He is the King of Israel; let him come down now from the cross, and we will believe in him. He trusts in God; let God deliver him now, if he desires him. For he said, 'I am the Son of God.'" And the robbers who were crucified with him also reviled him in the same way.[9]

Notice here that Matthew's Gospel says *both* of the robbers reviled Jesus. Luke, in his account, tells us more since after the crucifixion he went and interviewed as many people as he could who told them what they saw. Matthew was telling only what he saw personally; Luke was telling what many eye-witnesses saw, so he had a fuller story to tell. This is what Luke tells us."

Lily read the account out loud, while the others followed in their Bibles:

One of the criminals who were hanged railed at him, saying, "Are you not the Christ? Save yourself and us!" But the other rebuked him, saying, "Do you not fear God, since you are under the same sentence of condemnation? And we indeed justly, for we are receiving the due reward of our deeds; but this man has done nothing wrong." And he said, "Jesus, remember me when you come into your kingdom." And he said to him, "Truly, I say to you, today you will be with me in paradise."[10]

Everyone held their breaths after the reading. Till Lily continued, "Notice here that only *one* of the two criminals went to be with Christ in paradise. What did the one robber do to get him into paradise that the other did not do?"

"I'm not sure," Josh replied.

"Before I tell you that let me show you how helpless both the robbers were. They were hanging on crosses. They could not go and get baptized. They could not go and earn money to pay back what they had stolen. They could do *nothing* to save themselves, either from physical death, or from the consequences of their sins *after* death. They were completely helpless."

"Yet one of them went to paradise and the other did not!" Jason cried out, as if the fact amazed him.

"That's right!" his sister agreed.

"Yes," Lily continued, that is what I wanted you all to notice. I repeat the question I asked before, 'What did the thief who went to paradise do that the other did not? In order to accept the free gift of eternal life he had to do *four* things – the same four things we all have to do to receive the gift of eternal life. We can do nothing good to *earn* our salvation, but we can all do *those* four things."

"What are those four things?" Josh asked.

"Let's just follow the actions of the one who went to paradise, and we'll find out.

"First, he *changed his mind* about the way he acted toward Jesus. Together with the other thief he had reviled Jesus. Something; we don't know what, caused him to change his mind. To change his attitude. That is what it means to repent, to change your mind about how you've been living your life. It's the very thing Rick did when he realized his prideful actions had caused the death of that innocent family. He wanted nothing to do with that way of life any more. We all have things we have to change our minds about – like leaving God completely out of our lives."

"What is the next thing?" Lyn asked.

"Read what he said to the other thief: *'Do you not fear God, since you are under the same sentence of condemnation? And we indeed justly, for we are receiving the due reward of our deeds; but this man has done nothing wrong.'* He *confessed* his own sin. He *admitted* he had done wrong and deserved to die for his sins. That, also is what we all have to do to gain eternal life. That also is what Rick has done. He has admitted the wrong he has done."

"Now you're getting me excited," Jeanie said. "What is the third thing this robber did?"

"He *believed*."

"Is that all?"

"Now don't think that is an easy thing, Jeanie. Believing in Jesus, and that He had a kingdom, wasn't a natural thing under those circumstances. Jesus was hanging on a cross just as he was, yet he was willing to put his eternal soul into His hands. He believed that a man, all broken down, and hanging on cross, had the power to save him. When he did that, what was Jesus' answer to him?"

Josh read from his own Bible: *"Truly, I say to you, today you will be with me in paradise."*

"So that's all I have to do, Lily. I just have to trust Jesus to take me to be with Him when I die? Is that what we all have to do?"

"Yes, Jeanie, but not *exactly* all. There is one more thing the thief did that we all have to do to accept the gift of eternal life. He not only confessed his sin, repented and believed. He also made a public declaration, first to the other thief, and then to all who could hear him, that he was putting his faith in Jesus."

"You mean we can't keep it a secret."

"No, Rick, we can't keep it a secret and still be faithful to Him. Jesus made that very clear. In Matthew chapter ten, Jesus said: *'So everyone who acknowledges me before men, I also will acknowledge before my Father who is in heaven, but whoever denies me before men, I also will deny before my Father who is in heaven.'*[11]

"Jesus says the same thing just as clearly in the Gospel of Luke: *'For whoever is ashamed of me and of my words, of him will the Son of Man be ashamed when he comes in his glory and the glory of the Father and of the holy angels.'*[12]

It was as if everyone took a deep breath after that, and let it out.

"I want to do that," Lyn said. "I want to tell my friends at school I believe in Jesus."

"Me to," Jason echoed his sister, and before Lily could fully realize it, she had a whole roomful of believers around her. They had all put their trust in Jesus Christ. She looked over at Rick and saw his face aglow with his newfound faith. After seven years of prison, and overwhelming guilt, Rick Anderson had finally found redemption.

If Lily thought that was the end of the night's surprises, she was mistaken. Rick pointed toward her and said in amazement, "Lily! The blemish on your cheek has not just faded. It has completely *gone*!"

The Shadow

Heather Rawlings had begun to feel the same sense of danger Lily had spoken of, and it unsettled her. She was almost certain of *when* this unsettled feeling had begun to plague her.

True, she had been unsettled *before* she had learned to accept Rick Anderson's sincerity, and to see him as an object of God's mercy and grace. That unsettled feeling had been different then; more of a protective instinct over her best of all friends, Lily Cameron. The disappearance of the blemish on Lily's face, and Rick's conversion was incontrovertible proof of God's loving purpose toward the two of them.

The unsettled feeling and sense of danger Heather felt now was entirely different. She was certain she was being followed but could not identify anything but a vague sense of being watched. Perhaps her shadow was not doing so from nearby, but from a distance. A few times, turning suddenly to look behind her she had seen a man with a camera, but he was merely taking pictures of flowers, trees, and the scenes about him.

She had not seen him since, but the feeling of being followed never left her. Was it possible that someone with a telephoto lens on his camera could observe her from a distance? It was a foolish thought. Who in his right mind would do such a thing? Perhaps, though the one shadowing her was not in his right mind. There were all kinds of weird people in the world. What if she were the target of one of those? The thought of this frightened Heather like nothing had ever frightened her before. If she was indeed being followed by such a person, what could be his reason for targeting her?

Nothing good. Of that she was sure.

"Father," Lily said while gripping Rick's hand in her own, "I would like you to meet Richard Wadsworth Anderson, the man God has chosen to be my life mate." Her use of his full name feeling a little quirky, but somehow appropriate.

Angus Cameron gave his future son-in-law a searching look before returning his gaze back to his daughter, "I know he is, Lily. Far be it for me to question the Lord's choice, but tell me, what of the blemish you said was on his soul? I don't detect even the shadow of it in his eyes."

Rick spoke up, "It is gone, sir. I believed in the One Who died for me, and he took it away."

"As He has the blemish on my face, father. It seems God's purpose for the blemish has been fulfilled. Whatever lesson God intended for me to learn from it has been learned."

Angus swept his hand toward the couch and went to seat himself in his favourite chair, "Well, there is no need to stand in the middle of the lounge. We have much to discuss. Please take a seat."

Once seated they all lapsed into silence. Not an uncomfortable silence, but one in which each was aware that something significant was to transpire. The tension of it was in the air, only easing when Angus addressed first one, then the other of them, "Lily, you know the fading of the blemish is only the beginning of the battles you both shall face? And Rick, you should be aware that the gift of forgiveness you have received comes with a call to follow a Person, not a religion?

"Lily has explained that to me, sir. I have a lot to learn, but I am willing to follow Jesus for all he has done for me."

"Rick, God's time will come for you to marry Lily. When that time comes you will call me *father*. Until then, please call be Angus."

"Thank you sir… I mean Angus."

"Now let me give you a verse from the Bible you would do well to memorize and seek to apply to your life. It is found in Matthew chapter sixteen, verses twenty four and twenty five. *Then Jesus told his disciples, "If anyone would come after me, let him deny himself and take up his cross and follow me. For whoever would save his life will lose it, but whoever loses his life for my sake will find it.'*

"I am determined to do what you suggest, but there is another reason Lily and I are here, besides getting to meet you and gaining advice from you."

Angus leaned forward with a curious glint in his eye, "And what might that be?"

"I have come to request you teach my sister and her family the path of discipleship."

Angus looked surprised, "Why would you ask me? I am not a preacher. I am not ordained. Would it not be better to find a church for you all to attend? Where Lily attends would be a good choice."

Rick said earnestly, "Lily tells me you are the best Bible teacher she has ever encountered."

"A somewhat prejudiced view, I would think."

Lily spoke up, "There are several reasons, father why you are the best choice. First, Rick's family has never been to church in their lives, not even to get married. They were married by a Justice of the Peace. It would be something of a shock for them to be thrust into church life without preparation."

"Then it is not just my family that needs instruction," Rick added. "Jeanie has been sharing her faith with her neighbours. Several of them want to learn more. She has arranged for them to meet at her home in the hopes you will come to teach them. They are somewhat distrustful of what they call 'professional ministers." They want someone to explain things to them on a personal level before they venture into what they call *organized religion.*"

"Do you have another reason, Lily?"

"I've told you about the sense of danger that has come upon me at my own church. Rick and I have visited several churches. We have not had time to actually attend a service in each of them, but just entering each church caused us to feel it. I do not think it is the fault of any of the churches we visited. I rather think the enemy is targeting us *specifically.* I think, with your ministry of intercessory prayer you will be able to protect those who gather in Jeanie and Josh's home."

"You realize, Lily, what a burden of responsibility you are placing upon me, child."

"I trust no one else, Father."

"I will seek the Lord's guidance. That is all I can promise you."

"That is all we can ask," Rick replied.

Lily and Rick were walking along the Welland Canal Trail when Rick commented, "Your father is certainly an unusual man, Lily."

"That he is, Rick. I cannot tell you how privileged I have been to be raised by him. Without his counsel I may not have been able to avoid the pitfalls young women so often fall into. Especially in their teen years."

"I wish I had had such guidance. My parents seemed not to have had a clue of what life was all about, besides their interest in poetry, that is. They certainly gleaned some noble ideas from it, but it kept them from feeling a need to seek God."

"Your parents were not alone in that, Rick. Many find enough satisfaction in earthly pursuits that they don't feel their need of God."

"So, what does your father do now that he is retired?"

"People seek him out to give them counsel. He has quite a following. He refers them all to the only One who can meet their need, the Lord Jesus. You wouldn't believe how many he has led to the Saviour, but he always recommends them to attend churches he knows will give them sound teaching. He has never presumed himself qualified to lead a congregation."

"Which is why he seemed reluctant to take on the responsibility of teaching a regular gathering?"

"Yes, but I think this time he might just take it on."

"I certainly hope so, Lily. I know you could do it if you had to. You've certainly done a great job of explaining the Bible to us, but I think your father has a rare understanding. I would certainly count it a privilege to be under such spiritual guidance as your father can offer."

"I know my father quite well, Rick. If I am reading him correctly, you may very well find yourself under his tutelage very soon.

As they walked, they came to a bench and Lily suggested they sit for a while. Holding hands, the only concession they had made to the "no touching" phase of their relationship, and gazed across the canal at the opposite tree-lined bank.

Lily turned her head to take in Rick's profile as he continued staring over the water. Heather had been right. She and Rick needed to spend time together. The love Lily felt for Rick was something God had placed in her heart. It was a divine act. She knew love for her had been planted in his heart, also. Regardless, she knew they could not move forward on that fact alone. A relationship needed a solid foundation built on mutual respect, and not just the mutual attraction some called *chemistry*. Time to explore each other's worlds was essential.

The chemistry was not lacking. She had thought restricting their touching to holding hands would keep her emotions and her physical response to him, in check. It had not. At night she found herself remembering his touch, and the thrill his touch gave her. She lay awake, praying for purity of heart, and control over her thought life.

Gazing at him now she had to acknowledge he was extremely handsome. It had not been as evident before, while his eyes had been shadowed by guilt, and his shoulders bowed with the weight of the "crime" he had committed. Now, however, things were different. Now he had found forgiveness and an understanding of God's plan for his life, his whole demeanor had changed.

He still lamented the pride and drunkenness that had cost the lives of an entire family, but he knew he could leave that with God, who could see the whole picture and work all things together for the good.

Rick's pale grey eyes now showed a depth that seven years of prison had not only masked, but had a hand in creating. His jaw-line was strong with lips she could not but think of as kissable. His features were reminiscent of an artist's depiction of a Greek god. Just being near him stirred feelings within her she had never felt in the presence of any other man before.

"Lily, look. There in the trees," Rick's words shocked her out of her reverie.

"What? What are you seeing?"

"It's not easy to see, but I saw movement, and something else… the sun glinting off some shiny object. Lily, I think it must be a camera. Someone has been taking pictures of us."

Richard Wadsworth Anderson was having his own struggles. He and Lily had spent an entire week of the two weeks leave she had been granted, together. Every available moment had seen them in each other's company, getting to know as much about each, and of their pasts, as possible.

So what was his problem? Well, there were several. For one thing he did not think he could bear to hold her hand any more. Not because it was unenjoyable. Exactly the opposite. Holding hands was simply not enough anymore. He wanted to wrap his arms around her and kiss her, but knew their agreed upon strategy of slow discovery was for the best. They had simply not known each other long enough to wade into the waters of passion without drowning in them.

Lily was possessed of a purity he simply would not violate, but it was pure torture to keep his hands to himself. Perhaps it was best to keep his distance from her and desist from holding her hand, but that would be even more excruciating. He was five years older than she. He was virile, and she more desirable than he could ever have imagined. It would take nothing less than God's intervention to keep his hands to himself and his thoughts pure.

The other problem was the love thing. Those three little words, "I love you" must never be spoken between them till Lily felt it was God's time to say them. That however, did not mean the reality if it did not pulsate like a living thing when they were together. Lily had acknowledged her love for Rick to Heather. He knew this because Heather had confided it to him. Rick had admitted his love for Lily to Jeanie, and he suspected she had communicated this to her new best friend, Lily. It was in Jeanie's nature. She just could not have helped herself. So they both knew the love thing as a fact, but not as something that was to be spoken between the two of them. It was too soon, but not saying it seemed equally wrong. He wanted to say it; needed to say it.

Rick's third problem was Lily's, in his view, incomparable beauty. He had never felt her blemish diminished her looks, but its removal made him speechless with wonder. Heather's description "drop-dead-gorgeous" while dramatic, just did not cut it. Her loveliness, both in and out, was beyond description. This left Rick with a sense of unreality. It did not seem possible in a thousand years that he would ever deserve to be loved and cherished by such a one. How could he spend time in close contact with Lily and still think and act rationally? *By trusting in Me,* a voice in his spirit replied. *I will navigate you through this if you will just trust me.*

"We know what the deceived one has planned to besmirch the character of the chosen ones, and their friend, the loyal one," Andromeda said to Magnificence. "Is there any way we can prevent it?"

The Almighty and His Son have forbidden us to intervene in this instance" Magnificence replied.

"It just seems such a gross thing to do to such a pure one. It is like throwing a bottle full of black ink onto the pristine white of a bride's wedding dress. It just doesn't bear thinking about. Why would He-Who-Knows-All permit such a thing?"

"It is not for us to question, Andromeda. You know this. Angels have no way of comprehending the ways of the Almighty when it comes to His love for the fallen race of humanity. The Son's sacrifice to redeem them is beyond our understanding. We long to look into it, but it is hidden from us. Better just to accept that the All-Wise-One knows better than we do.

"Even those who are redeemed cannot plumb the depths of the Father's love, and His ways of dealing with them. The Scripture is clear about that:

'Oh, the depth of the riches and wisdom and knowledge of God! How unsearchable are his judgments and how inscrutable his ways!

'For who has known the mind of the Lord,
or who has been his counselor?"

'Or who has given a gift to him
that he might be repaid?

For from him and through him and to him are all things.
To him be glory forever. Amen.'"

"You are right, Magnificence. Such love is beyond our comprehension –
and beyond the comprehension of those upon whom it is bestowed."

CHAPTER TWELVE

Days of Wonder

"I remember coming here when I was a child." Rick said, but the only thing that stands out is its curious name. *Balls Falls* triggered strange images in my mind then. I pictured a zillion balls tumbling over the edge of a cliff; golf balls, billiard balls, even footballs. You get the idea."

Lily chuckled and squeezed Rick's hand, even as her own memories appeared vividly on her mind's eye, "I've been here many times, Rick. First with my parents before mom became ill, and then with my dad because it helped us to remember the good times we had enjoyed as a family."

"It must have been hard."

"It was, but not in a bad way. More bittersweet, with the mingling of sadness and gratitude for the life she had lived. We knew her suffering had ended and she was at last reaping the reward of placing her trust in Christ."

"Lily," Rick said, turning to gaze into the incredible blue of her eyes, "I feel like a small child. Since you explained how Jesus is my substitute and paid for all the evil I have done, I feel lost *and* saved at the same time."

"What do you mean?"

"Well, it is like I am standing on the beach with my feet in the ocean. There is such a sea of knowledge out there that I can never hope to fully comprehend. I know I've been forgiven, but I've only just got my feet wet. I feel both amazed by Christ's love for me, and intimidated by all I still need to know."

Lily took hold of Rick's hand again and they began to walk the trail winding through Balls Falls. It made its way through the woods and along the river bank on its way to the upper falls.

"Rick, the life of faith is a *journey*." She squeezed his hand as if to emphasize the word. "We cannot arrive at the upper falls except by taking one step at a time. You have taken the first step by trusting in Jesus. There are many more steps to take but you can't take them all at once. Don't try to understand everything at once, it will only confuse you."

"That makes sense. So, what is the next step?"

Lily was silent till they were standing at the upper falls, hearing the roar of vast amounts of water plunging into the stream below.

"You probably know by now Balls Falls is named after the Balls family. Jacob Ball was forced out of New York after the American Revolution because of his loyalty to the crown.

"After the war of 1812 his two sons were granted twelve hundred acres, which included the upper and lower waterfalls we are visiting today. Your childhood idea of zillions of balls flowing over a cliff reminds me of the many false ideas of what faith in Christ means. They are mere fantasies, just as the zillions of balls flowing over a cliff are fantasies. I think these falls represent something far more wonderful."

"What do you see when you look at these falls, Lily?"

Lily took a deep breath, her eyes shining with the thoughts passing through her brain, "I see the water in these upper falls, flowing into the depths below, as the endless mercy God offers all sinners. And it all flows from the suffering Christ endured on the Cross."

"Incredible word picture you are painting, Lily."

"I'm not finished. To me the lower falls represents the mercy and grace still flowing to our time in history, still available for those who believe."

"And I would imagine," Rick said with sudden insight, "the river below those falls speaks of God's mercy flowing into the future."

"Exactly right, Rick. God's love and mercy never stops flowing while human history continues. But let us continue on our way to the lower falls. There are others sights to see on the way."

The man fixed his gaze on his friend seated on the other side of the large oak desk.

"What progress have you made with the project I have asked you to accomplish?"

Draped languidly over the chair, his artsy demeanor unapologetic, his friend replied, "I have taken every possible picture of the three subjects from every possible angle I can think of." He reached for a large manila envelope propped against the leg of his chair. Placing it on his friend's desk he scooted it over to within his friend's reach.

The man opened the bulky package and spent some time going through the black-and white images. They were of such clarity and depth that left no question as to the identity of the subjects. He had expected no less from his friend.

"What more is to be done?"

The artist shifted in his chair, "I have to find suitable compromising pictures of nude groupings, and super-impose the faces of the subjects upon them."

"How long will it take?"

"Such images are not readily available, at least not in the groupings that will suit our purpose. A week. Maybe more."

"Will the manipulation of images be easily detectable?"

"Not initially, but if submitted to experts in the field, eventually."

"That is all I am asking. By the time that happens, the damage will have been done. After their reputations are destroyed, we can move to the final phase. Not one of them will escape the justice they deserve for their deeds."

The man expected his artist friend to rise and leave at this point. He did nothing of the sort. He seemed to be waiting for his response.

"What is it friend?"

The artist exhaled a breath, "I think. No, I am sure, I have found the perfect place to end the lives of these two – after their humiliation has been accomplished, that is."

"Pray. Tell me what you are thinking, my friend."

So, for the next half hour these two malevolent conspirators planned the demise of two of God's redeemed children.

When Lily and Rick arrived at the lower falls they had seen the lime kilns, and seen the picturesque Anglican Church that a stone plaque informed them had been moved there from Hannon, Ontario in 1974.

"I believe people have weddings here, now, so it is not just a monument."

Before Rick could curb his tongue, he blurted, "Perhaps we…"

Lily's face coloured, "Rick, you can't be suggesting…"

"Lily, I can't help it. We have the love. Surely you can't deny it. I know you felt it. Jeanie and Heather have revealed our secret. Why can't we say those three little words to each other?"

"I… I'm not denying it, Rick." She stared at the ground, afraid if she lifted her gaze to his the irresistible magnetism between them would draw them together and… And what? And they would cross over the line of propriety and… passion would flare between. That must not happen. It was too soon.

"Not yet, Rick. Not yet. Let us go look at the falls."

"This time she did not take his hand. She kept a distance between them and Rick felt he had made a monumental blunder.

They had stood by the stone wall skirting the gorge below and moved to the gristmill before Lily allowed Rick to take her hand again. She felt she needed to give him an explanation.

"Rick," she said, "it is not that I don't want to hold your hand. It is just that my father has taught me the dangers of youthful passion, especially between a man and woman who love each other – until marriage, that is. And we cannot discuss marriage yet. We have to wait for God's time."

"It's alright, Lily. I feel it too. Quite frankly, holding hands is not enough, but not feeling your hand in mine would be more excruciating torture than I could handle. All I can do is to trust God to reign in my desires so as not to displease Him – and dishonour you."

"I confess I have had to do the same, Rick. We will trust God to help us. Both of us."

The gristmill, where wool and fabric garments had been manufactured, was a long white building on the edge of a precipice. A wire fence extending from the end of the building to an outcrop of rock was meant to prevent visitors from going out onto the ledge. The fence-post next to the rock was wide enough, however, to allow someone thin enough to squeeze though if they so wished.

It turned out that Rick was one of those people who so wished.

"Please Rick, don't go out there. I'm sure it is a sheer drop to the bottom of the gorge."

"It's not as dangerous as it seems, Lily," he said as he squeezed past the post. "There is quite a wide ledge, and a concrete extension."

Lily stood and held onto the metal railing, shuddering as she imagined Rick slipping and plunging to the rocks below. When he at last came back through the gap she gave him a stern look and said, "Rick, please promise me you will never do that again."

Seeing the fear slowly leaving her eyes, he readily agreed, taking himself to task for unsettling her.

There was something so incredible strong about the way Lily stood by her commitments and held to her convictions. Yet there was a corresponding fragility to her as well. She was not like an implement of brass that could sustain endless blows without damage; she was more like a beautiful piece of china that could be shattered by a careless sweep of an arm, or cracked by being accidentally knocked against a wall.

It appeared even the thought of him being in danger had shaken her. The idea of being so cared for by such and incredible woman almost overwhelmed him. The contrast between the seven years of humiliation, and the undeserved favour he was now experiencing was almost too much to take in. Gratitude for God's goodness welled up within him.

As they moved back to the stone wall to take in the sight of the lower falls again, Rick saw a man with a camera. It looked expensive, with a large extended lens Rick guessed was telephoto, capable of taking close-up pictures from a distance. While the man was taking pictures of the falls, and other surrounding objects, an eerie sense settled upon him. He may have been taking pictures of *them*. He was sure of it.

Directing Lily's attention to the man, Rick said, "I think that is the man who took pictures of us from across the canal."

Lily's eyes grew wide with surprise, "How do you know?"

"I'm not sure. I just know."

"Why would he take pictures of us? We're just strangers to him. Unless he is just making a record of places and events to remember later. You know, for later enjoyment of his visit here."

"I don't think so, Lily. There was nothing casual about his picture taking at the canal."

"Rick, why are you being so suspicious?"

"Just a feeling I have, Lily."

She seemed to contemplate this for a moment, before saying, "Talking of feelings, you remember how I've had this sense of danger at work and at various places around St. Catharines?"

Rick nodded, "What about it?"

"I don't feel it here at all. I think we should make regular visits here."

"Fine with me," Rick said. *I don't really care where we hang out, as long as I can spend time with this incredible woman.*

Lily did not want these special times with Rick Anderson to end. She fantasized about a time, in the distant future, when they would never have to part again. That time would come she had no doubt, but it was critical it took place at the timing and pace God had ordained. Anything else could only lead to pain and disappointment.

Spending quality time with Rick was revealing two things to her; depths to his character she had only glimpsed before, and the intensifying of the physical and emotional attachment between them.

While he obviously wanted to wrap his arms around her in a passionate embrace, he had iron control over these urges. He respected the limits she had place upon their physical proximity. She felt it necessary, not only to protect *him* from crossing over from love into lust, but for herself as well. Her desire for him was as strong as his for her, she was sure. She was keeping a distance between them for both their sakes. She suspected he was not just bending to her wishes, but was acting from his own convictions as his relationship with the Lord grew.

Her love for Rick Anderson, though generated initially by an immediate act of God, was growing as she was gaining insights into his character. This was especially remarkable in that he had not grown up with the godly influences she had. His parents had been essentially godless. Yet at his core he was an honourable man, and she loved him for it. She squeezed his hand again to express wordlessly the thoughts going through her mind.

He squeezed back, and she wondered, as their eyes connected, how he could have become even more handsome in the space of only a few seconds.

Do human relationships usually progress at such speed?" Andromeda asked his companion.

"No," Magnificence replied, "but the Almighty is advancing things more rapidly for two reasons."

"And what may those reasons be?"

"Michael, that great prince, has revealed to me, and for you to know as well, that the onslaught against these two is going to increase to such levels as they will only have each other to commiserate with. The loyal one will provide some support, and the chosen one's father can intercede for them. Beyond that, the entire community will be against them. Only their mutual love will be able to sustain them. Apart, that is, from the Spirit's sustaining power."

"And the second reason?"

"The All-knowing One has called them to a calling that is destined to impact a certain part of the world in ways they cannot even begin to imagine. A great calling will require a great love to enable them to triumph together."

"The ways of the Almighty are indeed past finding out," Andromeda declared, unable to get his angelic mind to wrap around such wonders as God was working for these two, who were merely humans.

CHAPTER THIRTEEN

Humiliation and Rejection

When Lily returned to work on Tuesday morning after two weeks spent with Rick, it was with mixed feelings.

She loved her work, but the thought of spending whole days without him left her with an unfulfilled longing to be in his presence. Was this what true love did to a person? This see-saw of emotions between agony and ecstasy; longing to be with the one you love but having to endure separation. Imagining what being in love would be like, Lily had thought it would be seamless bliss. The reality was a patchwork of emotions, with insecurities and delights all blended together. Unsettled as she was feeling before she arrived at work, she was totally unprepared for what she was met with when she entered the doors,

For one thing, Carolyn, the former secretary was at *her* desk.

That was not supposed to be. Carolyn was only meant to stand in for her for the two weeks of her special leave, so she could be forgiven for the abrupt way she addressed the former secretary.

"What are you doing here?"

The mixture of emotions Lily read on Carolyn's face ranged between regret and disappointment, but mostly disappointment. Carolyn was a compassionate individual who always thought the best of her friends, and particularly of her fellow believers. Seeing disappointment from one she had almost idolized before was like a slap in the face – unexpected and stinging her sensibilities. Lily took a step backward under the force of it.

"What is the matter Carolyn? Why are you looking at me like that?"

Without preamble Carolyn said, "Pastor Jake wants to see you in his office. As she turned and proceeded down the hall to Pastor Jake's study she could feel the sympathy of this godly woman following her.

She stood outside the pastor's door in an attempt to calm herself and still the beating of her heart. What on earth could have brought about this reaction from a woman she admired? And what could the pastor want to discuss with her? At last the calm she sought settled on her spirit and she knocked on the door. At the pastor's "Come in!" she opened the door and entered.

Always before on entering the pastor's study she felt confident and welcomed. Now she felt the same disappointment that had come from Carolyn.

"You... you ... want to see me, pastor?"

"I do, Lily. Please be seated." The tone of his voice was tinged with regret, as though what he was about to discuss with her was the last thing in the world he wanted to talk about. Totally ignorant of what that might be, Lily felt mystified and nervous at the same time.

"Why would that be, Pastor?"

For interminable seconds' pastor Jake said nothing. When he did speak it was with reluctance, "I never expected this of you, Lily Cameron?" The use of her full name sounded strange to her ears. Only when her father was displeased with something she had done, did he use her full name.

"Expect what of me, sir?" The formal address corresponding to the formality of his use of her full name.

"You don't really know, Lily?"

"No, sir. I don't know what you could possibly be referring to."

"It seems the evidence of what you have done has been delivered to every pastor in St. Catharines."

"What could I possibly have done sir, to make it necessary to inform every pastor in St. Catharines?"

The look of total ignorance on Lily's face must have given the pastor pause. With a rather softened expression and tone of voice, he said, "You really don't know, Lily?"

Know what, sir?"

With a bewildered look on his face Pastor Jake muttered something she may not have heard, except for her senses being sharpened by the extreme situation she was in, "*Then, it may not be true. Lily may be innocent.*"

Taking a large manila envelope from his desk drawer, the pastor reluctantly slid it over to her.

"If you are as ignorant as you look, Lily, you will be embarrassed by what you find here. I hesitate to let you see them, but you won't understand what is going on unless you see them."

Keeping one hand firmly anchored to the desk she reached for the envelope, a feeling of fearful anticipation following the motion of her hand. She had to let go of the desk to open the envelope, and her trembling fingers almost could not accomplish the task. Eventually she managed, and half a dozen pictures spilled out onto the pastor's desk.

The images showed she and Rick in a variety of passionate embraces in public places. Seeing the pictures depicting what she and Rick had religiously avoided engaging in made her feel violated, and somewhat guilty. They had never actually embraced, but they had wanted to, though not in public.

Trying to comfort her, Pastor Jake said, "There is nothing really gross about these pictures, Lily, except their performance in public.

"They will, however, be seen by others as inappropriate behaviour by one with as spotless a reputation as you have. It will also, regrettably, cast a shadow over the testimony of this church. That is, if we don't deal with it the way people expect us to."

"You're saying you are going to fire me?"

Not, *fire* you, exactly. More like *letting you go* for the good of the Gospel."

"It *feels* like I'm being fired, pastor. You know how I love my work."

That is why I said we are not firing you. I've discussed this with the board, and they've agreed to pay your salary for three months, as a kind of 'leave of absence.'"

"So you don't believe I've actually done this, pastor."

"I don't know how these pictures came to be, but I suspect they are the result of what is known as 'photo manipulation.' Though why someone would go to so much trouble to destroy your reputation is a mystery. I and the board felt three months would give us, and you, time to prove these aspersions groundless."

Lily felt humbled by such evident faith being placed in her, "I thank you pastor, and the board, for believing me, and defending me – even before I knew I was being accused.

"I think, however, I need to assure you Rick and I have never engaged in the activities depicted in these pictures – either in public or private."

"I know that, Lily."

Lily continued as if the pastor had not spoken, "Rick and I have never done anything more than holding hands, but even that has been a challenge for us. We are in love, but we believe it happened too suddenly for us to proceed too quickly before getting to know each other. That is why I requested two weeks' leave. To spend some quality time together. Holding hands has left us with a dilemma. It would seem better not to hold hands at all, because of the desires doing so stirs within us. On the other hand, once having begun the practice, ceasing to do so leaves us both desolate. We have agreed to trust the Lord to keep our desires under control, while we enjoy the comfort Holding hands gives us."

"I have been in love, too, Lily. I understand."

Of course, Lily thought, it was the devil who was doing this to her, but he was not doing it alone. He had deceived, and possibly possessed, some human instrument to come up with such a scheme – and to put it into practice. She immediately began to pray for the perpetrator, or perpetrators, of such evil intent, *"Father, forgive them, for they do not know what they are doing"*

Lily's heart-beat slowed and a calm came upon her like nothing she had experienced before. *I will never leave you, or forsake you, Lily. All this will work out for good. Trust Me.* The inner voice was clear and distinct. She knew it was the voice of the Holy Spirit.

The pastor gave her a look that made her sure he did not believe the testimony of the pictures. But he *had* believed them – at first. Lily could understand that. The pictures were of such quality, any manipulation could not be detected, except by an expert's careful examination. It must have initially shocked the pastor to see those images before his habitual wisdom had kicked in and he realized they could not be true.

"I *know*, Lily. I know you did not do this, but I can't forgive myself for even *imagining* you could have engaged in such behaviour."

"It's alright pastor. These pictures were skillfully designed to deceive.

If I did not know these things did not happen, I would be tempted to believe them myself."

"I've heard of this before," Pastor Jake said, "I just never imagined anyone would use it in such a manner. It is called photo-manipulation, as I said before. I've seen examples of it from the Victorian era, pictures of a juggler juggling human heads. I saw one of the ghostly image of someone long dead standing behind a living person. Nothing I've seen, however, even comes close to the skill needed to create these images."

"So, pastor, what are you going to do now?"

A painful expression crossed Pastor Jake's features as he reached for the phone, "There's not a lot I can do about the big picture, Lily. These pictures have been spread to every pastor in the region. I think the board has made the right decision. It will give us time to try and correct this, without causing you to suffer financially while we do so."

He punched in some numbers. When his call was answered he said, "Carolyn, would you please come into my study right away." He replaced the receiver and they sat in silence till Carolyn appeared in the doorway.

"Carolyn, please come in and take a seat. We have a real problem to sort out. He took a deep breath and let it out slowly before declaring, "Lily is not guilty of engaging in such behaviour."

B... but..." Carolyn said as she settled herself into a chair. The pictures..."

"Are fake," Pastor Jake said, "skillfully wrought, for some inexplicable reason, to destroy Lily's reputation."

"How... how do you know they are fake?"

First, Lily denies it and I believe her. For Lily to do such a thing would be totally out of character. We owe it to take her word for it. She has never given us cause to doubt her before. Why should we disbelieve her now?"

Carolyn cast an apologetic glance toward Lily, "I... I'm sorry..."

"No need to apologize, Carolyn. These pictures are masterful examples of photo manipulation. Anyone would believe they are genuine."

"We can do something about the pastors who have received these pictures, Lily, and about the staff in this church. Carolyn, I want you to call a special staff meeting. There we can assure them of Lily's innocence in this matter, though I suspect none of them believe Lily capable of this behaviour in any case.

"Next I will draft a letter I want you to send to every pastor and denomination in the region, assuring them what measures we are taking, and of our total faith in Lily's character. I will also inform them what measures we are taking to deal with the situation. Lily's position is not being permanently terminated, we are just giving her, and us, time to deal with the fallout from this attack upon her character."

Carolyn turned to Lily, "Just be sure to get back after three months. I'm enjoying my retirement too much to stick around too long."

"I'll do my best, Carolyn, but it may not be something I have any control over."

Gratitude for such loving support welled up in her. Addressing both of them, she said, "I can't say I am not devastated by this pastor, but the love you are showing makes me feel I am part of a family.

"Because we *are*, family, Lily. We are all blood-bought children of God, and we must stand together when the enemy attacks us. An attack against *one* of us, is an attack against *all* of us."

The pastor paused and Lily thought he may want to say something more, but was hesitant about saying it.

"What is it, pastor?"

Lily, don't think I'm judging or anything, but I'm a little surprised at your choice of a life mate. You must know about his history, and the seven year jail term he served?"

"I know it pastor, but I must tell you God is restoring him, just as Nebuchadnezzar was restored, and King David after committing adultery – and the Prodigal Son who was welcomed back after wasting his living. Rick gave his life to Christ just over two weeks ago. His past has been wiped clean by the blood of Christ."

Pastor Jake looked duly rebuked as he said, "That's all I wanted to know, Lily."

"And pastor, I did not choose Rick Anderson to be my life mate, God chose him for me."

"I've been fired from my job," Heather lamented as the three friends drank tea together in Jeanie and Josh's kitchen.

They had decided not to meet at the coffeehouse, agreeing that a friendlier environment was called for.

Jeanie and Josh, and the small group of new believers meeting in their home, were of special comfort to them.

Rick said gloomily, "Social services have mentioned petitioning for the cancelling of my parole. Whoever took those pictures sent them to all the government agencies involved in setting the rules for my parole. I could end up back in jail."

"That's not going to happen," Lily said. "For one thing I don't believe the Lord will permit it now he is in the process of restoring you. For another, I don't think kissing your girlfriend, even in a public place, is a violation of your parole. They might not like it, but it does not constitute parole violation."

"My situation is quite different, Heather said gloomily. Pictures of me passionately embracing someone who is a total stranger to me, were sent to the heads of my company. "I'm not in danger of going to jail, but my chances of finding work are pretty much zero at this point."

"Any ideas what to do next?"

"I think I'll go visit an aunt of mine in Nova Scotia for a while. I hate to abandon you two, but I'm feeling uncomfortable in St. Catharines at present. I need to get away to a place where I can *breathe*."

"Don't worry about us, Heth. The two weeks I took off for Rick and me to get to know each other didn't seem to be enough. I almost hated to go back to work at the end of it. Now we have all the time we want. Whoever is behind this smear campaign has done us a favour."

"The Enemy's forces are gathering, Magnificence. All of them are concentrated around the two chosen ones."

"An assault against them is imminent, but do not despair, Andromeda. Re-enforcements will arrive soon. We will not have to act alone. The small army of intercessors is growing.

"The chosen one's father is indeed a mighty prayer warrior, though it is taking a toll upon him. Seeing his daughter so misrepresented in those pictures almost destroyed him. Even knowing the images were manipulated hardly made a difference."

"Yet he continues to pray and bring other intercessors into the fray."

"The Enemy made a tactical error, Andromeda. By shocking the sensibilities in such an extreme manner, he caused the opposite of the intended result. He did not reckon on the depth of this man's love for his daughter. His prayers became so much more intense and believing, they brought a host of new intercessors into the battle."

Do those intercessors know for what and whom they are praying?

"No, they do not, but they are nevertheless praying with inexpressible groaning, as the Spirit enables them to pray. The apostle Paul described this in his letter to the Romans: 'Likewise the Spirit helps us in our weakness. For we do not know what to pray for as we ought, but the Spirit himself intercedes for us with groanings too deep for words. And he who searches hearts knows what is the mind of the Spirit, because the Spirit intercedes for the saints according to the will of God.'[13]

"So," Andromeda said, "When the critical moment arrives we can act?"

"We can and will act, Andromeda, and so will a thousand angels of Light assigned to us.

CHAPTER FOURTEEN

Principalities and Powers

"I've heard of *The Morningstar Mill* many times," Rick said, "but I've never had a chance to come here before now."

"It's the perfect place for a picnic, with a variety of sights to see afterward, including the *Bruce Trail*."

"And this pond, and ancient gristmill, a waterfall, and a river I believe people swim in."

"Do you know its history, Rick?"

"Not really."

"Robert Chappell built the gristmill here at *Decew Falls* in 1872. He built it from stones laid by the previous owner, John DeCou, who also operated a mill here. It was called, *Mountain Mill*. The original mill was powered by a waterwheel, but Robert Chappell installed a turbine to power his mill."

"You've done your research, Lily."

"Actually, I cheated. There's a stone plaque over there that gives the history of this place. I read it while you were getting the picnic table set up."

"I'm sure this is not the first time you have read that plaque. You've been here before."

"Many times, but what interests me is the two different power sources employed by DeCou and Chappell."

"I have a feeling," Rick said, "I'm going to hear you draw a spiritual correlation between the two sources of power?"

"Brilliant deduction my dear man," Lily gave a comical rendition of a game show host, causing Rick to chuckle at her antics.

"You win the prize for the most intelligent man around."

Rick laughed again, "Since there is not another man to be seen around here, I guess I win for not having any competition."

Pulling herself back into a more serious mode, Lily explained, "The gristmill was first operated by *natural* means, a waterwheel, powered by the waterfall. Robert used a turbine, or dynamo. Both worked, but the turbine was much more powerful and efficient.

"We, too, can live our lives drawing from two sources, the *natural* or the *supernatural*. In Acts chapter one verse eight, Jesus promises we shall receive power when the Holy Spirit comes upon us. Now, the original word translated 'power' in that verse is *dunamis*, the Greek word from which we get the English word, *dynamic*, and *dynamite*. We can either fight life's battles with our natural human abilities, or rely upon the dynamic power of the Holy Spirit."

Rick gave her a discerning look, "Is there a point to explaining this to me, Lily?"

"Apart from the obvious one of explaining Scripture to you? Yes."

"What might that be?"

"Well, there's a Scripture verse I can't seem to get out of my head."

"I don't suppose it is the same verse I can't seem to get out of *my* mind, either, is it? But you go first."

"Okay, mine is from the book of Ephesians. It says:

'For we do not wrestle against flesh and blood, but against the rulers, against the authorities, against the cosmic powers over this present darkness, against the spiritual forces of evil in the heavenly places.'[14]

"Lily, that's precisely the verse that has been running through *my* mind for the past week. What do you think it means *both of us* being impressed with the same verse?"

Lily said seriously, "I think it means God is trying to tell us something, Rick. I think something is about to happen we need to be prepared for. I don't think whoever is targeting us, is done with us. *He*, or *they*, have made at least one attempt on our lives, violated our privacy, and ruined our reputations."

"So, what do you think they have planned for us, Lily?"

I think *they* are planning another attempt on our lives. They want to *kill* us, Rick."

"Which is why we need to rely upon the supernatural power of the Holy Spirit."

"*And*," Lily said with emphasis, "Pray like we have never prayed before."

"What if they don't go back to Balls Falls," the man asked his friend.

"Oh, they will," his friend replied. We have put so much pressure on them by destroying their reputations, they will seek a place to retreat to and 'lick their wounds,' so to speak."

"They have already gone to the Morningstar Mill for that reason. What's to prevent them from going somewhere else?"

Patience, my friend. Sooner or later they will go back to Balls Falls, and we'll be ready for them."

"I confess, I'm getting a little impatient. I can't wait till they pay for the death of that beautiful family. But you are right. Impatience could lead to a mistake, and we could be exposed before the deed is done."

"Exactly," his friend said, and rose to leave.

Angus Cameron let his gaze pass over the new believers gathered in the Johnson's living room.

All of them, including his future son-in-law, Richard Wadsworth Anderson, were trophies of God's amazing Grace, His undeserved favour bestowed upon unworthy sinners. Beside Rick, sat his own daughter, who had been the conduit through whom God had wrought this miracle. His chest swelled with fatherly pride. She was a stark reminder of her mother, bringing at once a sense of loss and gain. She had inherited, not only her mother's beauty, but also her faith and inner strength.

A pain twisted through him as he thought of the blemish on her face now gone, but a blemish on her character and reputation cast upon her by someone with evil intent. He nevertheless put his faith in the God of all Comfort that her reputation would be restored once more.

Angus shook himself free from these deliberations and gave his full attention to the small gathering of new believers.

He had never aspired to be a preacher or a pastor. At least, not in the conventional sense. He had always felt it was his lot to fulfill a humbler role. Sure, he taught Bible truth to individuals in his calling as counsellor, but he had not felt called to lead a congregation – until now. Lily and Rick's invitation had settled upon him with the force of a divine mandate. One he could not deny.

"Well," he said to those gathered before him, "it appears God has brought us together so you can fully understand the Gospel, and be built up in His most holy faith."

He took a deep breath, "To do that we must begin at the beginning. And the beginning is simply this: *all have sinned and fall short of the glory of God*. It is found in the book of Romans, chapter three, and verse twenty three. (ESV) He waited as those present tried to find its location in their Bibles. Lily helped a few seated near her.

"You see God is not just asking us to stop sinning," Angus continued. "He is demanding absolute perfection. The only way we can *earn* our own salvation is to *never ever have* sinned. To earn our own salvation we must *never ever have* sinned. Yet the Bile tells us we have *all* sinned. That means it is *impossible* to save ourselves. We are lost sinners. If we are ever to gain Heaven *Somebody Else* will have to do it for us. Somebody who has *never ever* sinned. That somebody is Jesus Christ."

And so Angus continued to lay a solid foundation of Biblical teaching in the minds and hearts of those gathered, who eagerly drank in what he said as desperately as those about to drown would cling to a life-raft. And as they drank it in, their eyes began to glow with understanding, and their expressions to light up with joy.

"The time is drawing near," Magnificence said as he swept an arm around him to encompass a great host of angelic beings. The thousand angels of light assigned to them had grown to ten thousand, due to the intensity of prayer being offered.

"But the battle will be joined long before then," Andromeda replied. "The Enemy's forces are gathering beyond anything I have seen before." He pointed to a dark mass of demons, filling the gorge where the chosen ones were intended to meet their death.

"Do not be concerned" Magnificence replied, "Such prayer has been offered as to give us the advantage. The Enemy has sought to stop that prayer, but

the chosen ones' father has prevailed and enabled the Spirit to call many intercessor's to join the fight. Victory is certain, though the enemy does not yet know it.

Magnificence raised his sword to call the angelic host to arms. Like lightning flashes, ten thousand swords like those Magnificence and Andromeda wielded, were drawn. In a moment the battle was joined in a spectacle earthly eyes have never seen, or can see.

Unearthly screams and triumphant shouts, albeit only discernable in the supernatural realm, echoed across the entire expanse of the heavens.

There was one man, however and perhaps several of the other intercessors, who were made aware of something unusual going on in the supernatural realm. That man was none other than Angus Cameron, the father and future father-in-law of the chosen ones.

Angus Cameron became aware of the heavenly conflict by a stirring in his spirit that brought him involuntarily to his knees.

It began at first as a gentle movement in his spirit, then grew in intensity till all he could do was groan into the carpet where he had fallen. Though recognizing this as the promised inexpressible intercession of the Holy Spirit through him, he had no idea what particular need he was praying for.

He could, however, guess.

His guess was more instinct that speculation.

Lily and Rick were in danger. The thought became a certainty, and he realized he was wrestling with forces beyond the earthly realm, a familiar Scripture passing through his mind:

'For we do not wrestle against flesh and blood, but against the rulers, against the authorities, against the cosmic powers over this present darkness, against the spiritual forces of evil in the heavenly places.'[15]

After an hour of such wordless intercession Angus felt a thrill of victory pass through him. He rose to his feet. He knew that now, whatever danger had threatened Rick and Lily – was gone.

"It was a good idea to come here again, Rick. Just walking the trails and exploring the woods along the way is calming. Losing my job, and our reputation hasn't been easy."

"*Your* reputation, Lily. I lost mine a long time ago. I'm willing to bet not many of those who really know you will believe the charges, or the rumours."

"That's the thing about rumours, Rick. People may not be entirely convinced of my guilt, but a seed of doubt will have been planted in their minds. The suggestion that I *may* have done those things was enough to take my job from me, at least temporarily, and you and I have been getting suspicious glances from people I know, and even from strangers. Pictures of us have been plastered all over town."

Rick took a deep breath, "How much is this really bothering you, Lil?"

Lilly squeezed his hand, "Not as much as you might think, Rick. For one thing, people said even worse things about Jesus. They said he cast out demons by Beelzebub, the prince of demons, so I am in good company. I am content to leave my reputation in the hands of my Lord. He has promised to work out all things for my good, if I love Him, and I *do* love Him, Rick.

"There is also something else I've been longing to do since I was quite young, and this may just be God's time for me to pursue it."

"And what may that be?"

Lily stopped in the path and gave Rick a searching look, "To become a missionary. To Africa."

"Really?"

"Really. There is a Bible College in Kitchener" She took both Rick's hands and asked seriously, "What do you think of that, Rick? How would it affect our relationship?"

Their faces were only inches apart when he replied, "Lily, I've not shared this with you before. I've only been a believer for little more than a month, but I've been having similar thoughts. The Gospel message you shared with me and my family has so transformed us, a longing has been born in me to share it with others."

"Really?"

"Really." They laughed at the exact same questions they had asked each other only a moment before, and resumed their stroll down the path.

"I'm just not sure if becoming a missionary in Africa is just what *I* want, or if it is the Lord who is prompting me."

"We'll just have to pray about it then, won't we? The Lord has promised to guide us, so we don't have to stress about it. Just wait for Him to lead us."

As they approached the small Anglican Church near the end of the trail, Rick stopped and gazed once more into Lily's eyes, "Lil, what if this is God calling *us* to be missionaries *together*? Social Services don't hold out much hope for me getting a real job, with my record and all. Going to Bible College would solve that problem, with only one more problem remaining."

"What problem would that be?"

"Lily, I don't think I could go to Bible College with you, and not be married to you."

"Rick…"

"Lily, think about it. Do you believe God brought us together?"

"Yes, but…"

"Lily, do you *love* me? And don't evade it this time. You've already admitted as much to Jeanie and Heather. Do you love me?"

"Y…yes. I do love you Rick but…"

"And I love you. We can do the 'getting to know each other' thing after we are married. We'd be working together toward one goal, united in every way."

"Rick, everyone tells me the first year of marriage is challenging enough. To do so while studying will be adding even more pressure."

"So you *are* considering it, Lily. I can see it in your eyes. Just promise me you will pray about it. If the Lord says yes, we can be married right here at *Balls Falls*, in this little church."

"Rick…"

"Lily, I am going to kiss you.

And he did.

Later, they stood silently gazing at the lower falls, alone. The sun was going down and most everyone had gone home.

Lily could not get the kiss out of her thoughts. It had felt… right. She had not expected it to. She had expected the kiss to stir feelings of guilt within her, which was why she had insisted on not going beyond the holding of hands.

To her surprise no guilt followed the kiss. The talk of marrying sooner than later, and going to Bible College together had shifted the dynamic of their relationship. It felt like they were engaged, though no engagement ring was in evidence. Being engaged made a kiss the most natural thing in the world.

The kiss had felt so right she knew she would not have to pray about marrying Rick and going to Bible College with him. She had felt the Lord's touch on her spirit, like a benediction.

That was not, however, all she had felt.

Desire and longing had accompanied the kiss, and like Rick, she knew she could not go to Bible College with him, and not be married to him. She turned to him and said, "Rick, I will marry you, just as soon as we can sort out the details of going to college."

Rick kissed her again.

Turning from the railing, now intent on leaving Balls Falls and heading home, Rick and Lily skirted the grist mill and came up short. A man with welding goggles, and a welding torch, was almost done cutting the guard fence down.

"Wh… what are you doing?" Lily asked, almost breathless with the shock of seeing nothing to prevent anyone from falling over the edge into the chasm below.

"People could still get around the fence," the man said reasonably, "We will replace this fence with something much safer."

His use of the word "we", and something in the man's demeanour, rang alarm bells in Lily's brain.

The man in the welding goggles rose and grabbed hold of Lily's arms. She was vaguely aware of a man in a mask standing behind Rick. Before either of them could take action, the two strangers propelled them toward the edge of the chasm, and threw them over it.

CHAPTER FIFTEEN

Dramatic Events

At last the demonic host was driven back and Heaven's angels formed a ring around the chosen ones to keep the demons at bay. "Could we not prevent the deceived ones from carrying out their wicked deed?" Andromeda asked.

We are forbidden to do that," Magnificence replied. "The Almighty is creating a situation in which the deceived ones will be forced to acknowledge that they are not been led by God, but the evil one."

"Why would He do that? Would it not be simpler to just remove the threat altogether. There would be no need to deliver the chosen ones at all."

"I cannot understand it all myself, Andromeda, but it has something to do with the Son's declaration when He walked the earth, that he had not come to destroy life, but to save it. Apparently, one of the deceived ones is to be offered mercy. The other may already have rejected that offer.

"It is indeed past comprehension that the Father, Son, and Spirit would not destroy the deceived one for his evil deeds."

"Bear in mind he was deceived, Andromeda. He thought he was being called to do what he did by God Himself. What is about to happen now has been designed to expose that lie. The chosen ones must be seen to go over the cliff, or he will harbour doubts God Himself has delivered them."

"Well, that moment has arrived. There they go over the cliff."

"I'll go for the girl. You deliver the other chosen one."

Like a flash of light Rick and Lily, about to crash on the rocks below, were borne up on angels' wings.

Lily's scream seemed to echo off the walls of the chasm. The fall seemed to take forever, for a million thoughts passed through her mind on the way to the bottom.

Among them was the sweetness she would be missing now that she and Rick would never be together in wedded bliss. The two kisses they had shared had opened up a vista of future possibilities she had never even imagined before. Now that future would be dashed on the rocks below.

The thought right on the heels of that one was that Heaven would fully compensate for any of the losses she might have suffered on earth. She would see Jesus, the lover of her soul, and that thought banished from her mind any sense of loss her death might have suggested.

It was at that point in her lightning fast deliberations she felt arms close around her. A voice spoke in her mind: *Do not fear, Lily Cameron, for you are greatly loved. The Father, the Spirit, and the Son have great plans for you and Richard Wadsworth Anderson.*

In an instant, her eyes were opened and she saw the being who was bearing her upward. Nearby she saw another angel, in whose arms her future husband was being borne. The expression on his face must have reflected her own – one of mingled shock and disbelief. Not *unbelief*, just *disbelief* that something so wonderful could be happening to them.

And then the momentous event was over, and they were placed safely away from the cliff top on solid ground.

Rick and Lily hardly had time to adjust to their deliverance before they were confronted with a scene almost as dramatic as the experience they had just passed through.

The two men who had thrown them over the edge of the cliff, still unidentifiable due to the mask and welder's goggles, were screaming. No, what was coming from their vocal chords was not screaming, but *wailing*. It was what Rick and Lily later thought might issue from the throats of the damned.

Both men stood as if welded to the spot by the welder's torch still in the hand of the one who had cut down the fence.

Rick and Lily were likewise unable to move, till the men were suddenly released from their immobile state, and fled from the scene as if the hounds of hell were close at their heels.

The first thing Rick did after their attackers were gone, was to wrap his arms around Lily as if he never intended to let her go. "I guess," he said into her ear, "our destinies are linked. There is no longer any need to delay preparing for a wedding."

"I guess not," Lily whispered back, "but I do think there is an immediate need for you to let me go. Holding me like this is stirring things in me I'd rather not be feeling right now."

Rick let her go so abruptly she stumbled backward, till he gripped her hands, preventing her from falling, "I… I am *so*, sorry Lily. I didn't realize…"

Lily took a deep breath to calm herself, "It… It's alright Rick. We've just been delivered from death by angels. It's not your fault. It is just my reaction I was concerned about. Until we are married we'll just have to be careful not to indulge in embraces like that."

"I know, Lily. I'm sorry." He looked over his shoulder at the setting sun. "We have to leave before it gets dark, and the gates to the park are closed."

Still in somewhat of a dream state from their miraculous deliverance, and from the intimate embrace they had just shared. They hurried to Lily's car parked near the entrance, just in time to exit before the gate was closed and locked.

As they drove home they sat in silence, busy with their own thoughts. It dawned upon Lily she had just agreed to marry Rick Anderson, after little more than a month after meeting him. She could only imagine what Rick was thinking just now. And what he must be feeling. She sighed with mingled astonishment and excitement.

Life was certainly going to be different from now on.

Pastor Andrew Wheller could not stop the shaking of his limbs.

It was a wonder he had been able to drive home without ending up in a ditch somewhere. His friend, Roland Mills was in an even worse state than he was, so letting him drive was a no brainer.

After dropping Rollie off at his place, he was finally able to make it home and park in his own driveway. He managed getting from his car to the front door smoothly enough, but getting his key into the key-hole was an ordeal. His hands were shaking so violently it took several attempts before he was able to turn the handle and stumble into his home.

Where to go now.

Andrew Wheller's home had always been a sanctuary to him, but no more. He had no wife since his near obsession with what he saw as his "calling" had precluded any forays into the dating world. So, at the age of forty three, and the most devastating crisis in his life, he was alone.

Not *alone*, exactly, for he had his swirling thoughts and the realization he had been wrong. No, much worse than wrong. He had been *deceived*, and under that deception had been guilty of murder – several times.

He at last made it to his study and sat behind his humongous oak desk and tried to make sense of what he had witnessed barely an hour ago.

Up to the point when he and Rollie had thrown Lily Cameron and Rick Anderson off the edge of the cliff he had been firmly convinced he was doing *God's* work. He had been engaged in bringing justice in situations where the justice system had failed.

When, however, Lily and Rick had miraculously appeared at the top of the cliff, it had become shockingly clear to him God was working *against* him, and not *with* him. Only God could have wrought that miracle of deliverance. For a split second of time he had actually imagined he had seen two angels bearing them up and depositing them on solid ground.

If his eyes had not been deceiving him, it meant he had *not* been working under the inspiration of the Almighty. Even if he had not seen the angels, there was no denying their two victims had *not* perished. So he had *not* been called to do what he had done by God himself, but by – the devil. He had been lied to by the father of lies. He had been drawn into the net of deception.

There was no doubt that Andrew Wheller was sincere in his beliefs, but the devil had taken that sincerity and twisted it to accomplish his own ends.

After several hours of wrestling with what his next course of action ought to be, and praying like he had never done in all of his life, he finally knew what he had to do.

He had to confess it all – but not yet. He had several things he had to do before he went to the police. And there was a certain someone he had to speak to first.

In the editorial of the local newspaper.

My editorial this week will take the form of a letter received from an anonymous source.

I have wrestled with whether or not to publish this letter, and decided to do so for one reason: the writer promised to confess to the things implied in it after a three month delay.

I have contacted the police, and because they have been unable to trace its source, and because the writer seems to be sincere, have agreed to allow the letter's publication.

So, here it is, without any editing, or changes made:

"I want the city of St. Catharines to know, and a few individuals in particular, that I have been guilty of several crimes, a number of murders among them. I know I am shocking you, but only a full and public confession will suffice if I am to receive cleansing and forgiveness for what I have done.

"I am delaying a full confession to the police for three months, because I want to seek godly counsel to prepare me for a life sentence in jail.

"There is, however, one confession that cannot wait. I was the one behind the besmirching of the reputation of a young woman of pure and exemplary life-style. Her name is Lillian Cameron, known as Lily to her friends. At the same time I besmirched the name of her boyfriend, Richard (known as Rick) Anderson. Though he has spent time in prison for vehicular manslaughter, he experienced a spiritual transformation and is now pursuing a life of godliness. Their best friend, Heather Rawlings, was also a victim of my poisonous accusations.

"I had pictures taken and manipulated to show them in compromising situations. These I sent to all the churches in St. Catharines, and to their place of work, to have the two young ladies fired from their jobs, and to ensure Rick Anderson never found a position during his probationary period.

I sincerely apologize for my reprehensible behaviour in this regard, and regret the negative impact I have had on this community at large.
Signed,
Deeply repentant.

"You must be completely out of your mind, Roland Mills spat at Andrew over the expanse of his desk. "You can't believe this drivel," he slammed the newspaper with Andrew's confession displayed, "will do any good. It will most certainly send you to prison for life. Almost certainly, I will end up there, too."

"I won't involve you, Rollie."

Rollie scoffed, "You're living in a fantasy world, Andrew. Once the police know who you are, and what you have done, it won't take them long to investigate your friends and acquaintances, though I think I am your only real friend. I'm not sure I can even be a friend to you anymore. Not after you doing something so stupid. They'll soon find out it was *I* who took and manipulated those pictures. I'll go to jail, even if they don't find out the murders I committed in pursuit of justice."

"Rollie, don't you think what we have been doing is wrong?"

"No, no, no!" Rollie shouted. We were doing God's work by making people pay for their crimes."

"And you don't think what we have done is a crime in itself?"

"No, I do not. We have been doing *God's* work. And Andrew, consider this. You have just made an enemy of me. If we ever meet in prison, just watch out!" So saying he stormed out of Andrew's office, and a minute later Andrew heard the roar of a truck engine, and the scattering of driveway stones as Rollie left, most likely never to return.

Angus Cameron moved swiftly from the kitchen where he was preparing his lunch at the urgent pounding on the front door. He could not have been more surprised to see Andrew Wheller, pastor of the Southside Community Church standing on the front porch.

"May I come in," Andrew said abruptly as he swept past Angus to stand like a pillar of salt in the centre of the living room.

"You seem upset, Andrew."

"No, I am *not* upset, Angus. When the neighbour's dog barks too loudly. I am upset; when members of my congregation won't greet me at the door, I am upset. No, Angus, I am *not* upset. I am angry – at myself. And confused. How could I have got it wrong for all these years?"

"What do you mean, Andrew? What have you got wrong?"

Instead of answering directly, Andrew took the newspaper in his hand and dropped it on the coffee table, "Have you read this editorial?"

"Yes, but what has that got to do with you?"

"Quite simply, Angus, "*I* wrote that letter. I was the one who destroyed your daughter's reputation, and that of her boyfriend. I even attempted to kill them both – twice."

Angus Cameron was not a man who could be easily shocked, or emotionally devastated. This revelation, however, from a man he had long respected, was so stunning as to rob him of both speech and logical thought. Till a full minute has passed.

The idea the man before him had been the source of the danger lurking over Lily at first stirred natural feelings of anger, then desire for revenge, followed by consternation, and finally by compassion.

He took a deep breath and said, "Andrew, I think we had better sit down. I want you to start at the beginning and tell me everything that has happened since you first felt you were "called" to be an avenging angel, right up to the present day. I want to hear all of it. Leave nothing out."

It took over two hours, Angus's lunch growing cold on the kitchen table till at last the questions and answers had been exhausted and the two men sat in silence. The enormity of the revelations settled on both men, each in his own way.

"So what are you expecting of me?" Angus asked at last.

"First of all, explain to me where I went wrong. When was I deceived enough to the extent of perverting the Gospel message into something entirely different?"

"What else do you want of me?"

"Angus, there is a *reason* I delayed my confession to the police for three months. I want you to re-instruct me in the true message of the Gospel. I don't want to get it wrong this time. I want to meet with you daily while you help me lay a solid foundation of what the Bible really teaches about sin, Grace, and redemption. Once I am fully instructed I will go to prison for life, but with a new mission."

"What is that mission, Andrew?"

"To spend the rest of my days locked in with lost men, in a position to share with them the Gospel of grace and mercy. Will you help me in this, Angus? But before you answer, let me refer you to a passage in Scripture you must know very well, and fits my situation."

Taking a New Testament from his jacket pocket he turned to the book of Acts and read: *Now a Jew named Apollos, a native of Alexandria, came to Ephesus. He was an eloquent man, competent in the Scriptures.*[25] *He had been instructed in the way of the Lord. And being fervent in spirit, he spoke and taught accurately the things concerning Jesus, though he knew only the baptism of John. He began to speak boldly in the synagogue, but when Priscilla and Aquila heard him, they took him aside and explained to him the way of God more accurately.*[16]

"I have been preaching what I thought was the true Gospel message sincerely and eloquently. I need you to explain the way of God to me more accurately. Will you do it, Angus?

Without hesitation Angus said, "I will, Andrew. I surely will."

CHAPTER SIXTEEN

Significant Events

Lily made her way to the secretarial desk where she had worked for over two years, and where she had always found the work satisfying and fulfilling.

Caroline greeted her with exuberance, and a welcoming smile, "Oh, Lily! I can't tell you how happy I am to see you. I can't *wait* to get back to my retirement."

The excited look on the super-secretary's face caused Lily some misgivings. She hated giving Carolyn her latest news, "Carolyn I'm afraid I have to tell you I am not coming back."

"N… not coming back?"

The expression on Carolyn's face would have been amusing, had it not looked so tragic.

"B… but…"

"I hate that my good news has evoked such a negative reaction from you."

"Good news?"

"Carolyn, I am going to get *married*. And that is not all. Rick Anderson, my fiancé, and I, are preparing to go to Bible College for three years, and then to the mission field – to Africa, South Africa."

"You are what? Lily, now that your reputation has been cleared you can come back. Everyone is talking about the editorial in the newspaper. You're free to come back to work, now."

Lily good naturedly put on a hurt expression, "Aren't you happy for me? Can't you at least be glad God has given me a new calling? And a soon to be – *husband*?"

Carolyn's face broke out in smiles, "Of *course* I am, silly. I'm just being selfish I've been so anticipating your return, it initially shocked me, that is all."

"I'm just teasing you. Of course you're glad for me. And I'm sure Pastor Jake will find a replacement for me soon enough, and you can go back to your retirement."

"That might not be as easy as you think, Lily. By all accounts, secretarial work is your superpower."

"An exaggeration, I'm sure. I am, however, here to see Pastor Jake."

"Of course you are. I'll ring through to him right away."

Five minutes later Lily was seated once more across from her former employer, remembering, quite vividly when she had last sat in this chair. The pastor had shown her pictures showing her and Rick in less than acceptable embraces in public, or private, for an unmarried couple. The pictures had been sent to every church in the city. Pastor Jake had believed she had not been involved in what the pictures suggested. Instead of firing her, he had arranged for a leave of absence, with full pay. The editorial in the newspaper had absolved her and cleared her name, but that did not take away from the huge favour Pastor Jake had extended to her.

She owed him. How could she leave him high and dry, and disappoint Carolyn who desperately wanted to get back into retirement? She now knew she could not do that. She would have to revise her plans.

"Carolyn tells me you are soon to be married. She also tells me you and your new husband intend to go to Bible College to prepare for missionary service."

Carolyn had no doubt called and given Pastor Jake this information in the short time it had taken Lily to walk from the secretarial desk to the pastor's study. Given the kind of secretary Carolyn was, she could pack a lot of information into a very short time.

"That is correct, Pastor. I am going to get married, and Rick and I are planning to prepare for missionary service in Africa."

"So, who is this 'Rick' you plan to marry, though I suspect it must be Richard Anderson, the man who spent seven years in prison for vehicular manslaughter."

"It is he I plan to marry, pastor."

Pastor Jake sighed, "Lily, I can't say I do not have misgivings about you marrying that particular man, and after such a short acquaintance. I am, however, not going to insult you by asking you if you are sure. You have no doubt consulted with your father, and I have too much respect for him to counteract any counsel he may have given you. And I am sure you have not neglected to seek God's will on the matter."

"That I have done, pastor."

"Alright then, Lily. Carolyn also tells me you do not intend to come back to work. It will, however, take time to be accepted at any college you may apply to, so with that in mind I have one request of you. I would like you to return to work for the three months we had originally planned to support you for on a leave of absence. That will give us time to search for someone to take over your position after you leave. The new school year for most Bible colleges is in September, a little over three months from now. That would also free Carolyn to go back into retirement."

Feeling a little ashamed she had not figured these things out for herself, Lily said, "I would be happy to do that, Pastor. It is the least I can do for all you have done for me. And for taking my word for it when my integrity was in question."

The pastor waved away the implied praise for his actions, "What college do you and Richard plan to attend"

Lily mentioned the Bible College in Kitchener her father had recommended.

"A good choice. How do you plan to cover the costs?"

"I have some savings, and my father has promised to contribute a little."

"Leave that with me, Lily. I take it your fiancé has nothing to contribute?'

"His sister and husband may contribute a little, but otherwise, no."

"As you know, Lily, the church has a budget designated to support missionary endeavours. I'll present your needs to the Mission Board. Perhaps we can be of some help to you as well."

"I can't begin to thank you enough, pastor. In the next three months I will endeavour to express that gratitude in the way I serve you and the mission of this church."

"I am sure you will, Lily. I have not even a sliver of doubt about that."

On her way out Lily took a great deal of pleasure in informing Carolyn of her new decision, "I'm coming back, Carolyn – for three months. I am sure Pastor Jake will be able to find someone to replace me in that time."

Carolyn's smile, if it could have been connected to a power grid, could have provided electricity for the city of St. Catharines for an entire week.

Rick Anderson had requested an interview with Angus Cameron while Lily went to inform the church of her new plans, and to tender her resignation.

Angus left Andrew Wheller in the kitchen to search the Scriptures, and to read the works of some classic writers dealing with the central message of the Bible.

His house was only a two bedroom affair, with no basement. Lily had one bedroom, and he had the other. So one corner of that bedroom designated as his study.

Angus took Rick in there to address his concerns, for he sensed that young man was somewhat troubled.

When they were seated Angus asked, "So what is troubling you, Rick?"

"Not *troubling*, exactly, but I do have some concerns."

"And what might they be?"

"I know you have never expressed opposition to Lily and me getting married, but I also know that our brief acquaintance must have crossed your mind, and been a concern to you, more than once."

"That it has, my lad."

"So, I am here to answer any questions in that regard, and to formally ask for her hand in marriage."

"This may surprise you, Rick, but I have no hesitation in granting it."

Surprise was the least of the expressions that crossed Ricks face. More like consternation – and disbelief.

"You were expecting me to list my reasons why marrying Lily is not a good idea, weren't you? You thought your time in prison and your brief acquaintance would be reason enough for me to deny you?"

Rick's nod was enough of an answer.

"There are several reasons, Rick, why none of that matters.

"The first is that Lily loves you, and believes God wants you to be together. She is not a flighty girl. The faith of her mother resides in her, a faith that does not expect everything to run smoothly. Her mother,

Madeline, remained strong in faith even through years while she was enduring the ravages of cancer.

"Lily would not have agreed to marry you without, above all else, seeking God's will. She also sought counsel from me as well.

"The second reason is that I was intimately involved in the battle raging in the heavens surrounding the two of you. The fact that so much angelic and demonic activity has surrounded you, convinces me your destinies are linked. If God intends for you to be together, who am I to object. Only, do not *ever* forget how great a responsibility God has placed in your hands in making Lily your wife. As the Scripture declares: *'Husbands, love your wives, as Christ loved the church and gave himself up for her…'"*[17]

It was clear from the expression on the young man's face that this speech had taken all the wind out of his sails.

"I am totally and completely blown away by this, sir. I can only assure you I will do everything in my power, and with God's help, to fulfill those obligations, sir."

"I am sure you will, lad, but I sense there is something else troubling you."

"Yes, sir, there is. Lily deserves to have an engagement ring, and a wedding ring. I have, however, no resources at present."

Angus slapped a reassuring hand on Rick's shoulder, "That, my lad, is a problem that can be easily resolved." Opening a drawer in his desk, Angus withdrew a small box and opened it. Set in a velvet cushion were two rings – an engagement ring, and a wedding ring.

"They belonged to Lily's mother, and I know she would want Lily to have them. I know because she told me so, And asked me to keep them for her. Problem solved."

Magnificence said to Andromeda, "The immediate crisis is over for these two, though there will be some challenges while they prepare themselves for the Almighty's plan for their future lives."

"True, but then our care for them will pass to others. By all accounts the challenges they will face in South Africa will be ten times what they have faced before. Besides that will be the child that will be born to them."

"And several others."

"I do confess, though, I will miss being directly responsible for them. They have been rather unique among the charges assigned to us in the past."

"They certainly, have, "Magnificence replied. "They certainly have."

"It is *so* good to have you back, Heth. And to hear you have your job back."

"Oh, I guess that editorial in the newspaper was what did the trick. My bosses were *so* apologetic. In fact it has all worked out for good. I've actually been offered a promotion. Not sure I'm going to accept it, though."

"Why ever not?"

"Well, that is the other good news I have for you. The position will require a lot of overtime, and I may be needing that time for more pleasant activities"

"I can't wait to hear it."

"I'm not sure I should tell you, Lil. Just in case it doesn't work out."

"You can't do that to me, Heth. You can't dangle some delicious news in front of my nose, and then withhold it from me."

"Oh, alright. "I'll tell you, but don't you *dare* laugh at me if nothing comes of it."

"*Heather*, you know I would never do that."

"I'm just nervous is all. And a little suspicious that it is just too good to be true."

"What *is* it Heth? Out with it."

"Heather leaned back in her chair, took a sip of her coffee, and said, "Well, you remember the guy I was mooning over all last year?"

"You mean Luke Richards. The guy you said didn't even know you existed."

Heather blushed. Well, it seems he *did* notice me. He was just shy. He didn't think he deserved someone like me. Can you believe that, Lily? Luke Richards, that gorgeous blue-eyed, Greek-god look-alike, doesn't think he deserves someone like me?"

Lily grabbed hold of Heather's hand, the one that was not crushing her empty paper coffee-cup, and stared directly into her eyes. "Heather, I hate to say, 'I told you so,' but I *told* you so."

"I know, Lily, I just didn't believe you."

"What about now, Heth?"

"I think I believe you now, Lil. I asked Luke why he felt drawn to me rather than all those girls in our young adults group, who are much prettier than I am."

"What did he say?"

"He said he was looking for someone whose beauty was more than skin deep."

"Like I said. I *told* you so."

"I also asked him if he would come with me to your wedding, and he said, 'Yes.'"

Lily was alone with Rick in Jeanie and Joshes living room.

For some strange reason, after gathering in the living room to have tea and cookies, all but Rick himself had made excuses, saying they had something important they had to do, and left them alone.

Lily could feel the atmosphere as thick as treacle, as if some significant event was about to transpire, and was just waiting to descend upon them. She was just about to break the silence when Rick moved in front of her and fell down on one knee. From his trouser pocket he took a small box, and her breath caught in her throat. She already knew what that little box signified. She had already told Rick she would marry him, but there had been no ring. She wondered how he could have afforded to get her one now.

"Lily," Rick said breathlessly, "I know you said you would marry me, but I have not asked you formally, and I have not given you a ring to make it official." He opened the box and there, resting in blue velvet, was not one ring, but two – an engagement ring, and a wedding ring.

And she recognized them both. They had belonged to her mother.

"How…"

"Your father gave them to me, Lily. He said your mother had made him promise he would give them to the man you were to marry, so you would have them to remind you of her."

Taking the engagement ring from the case, he gently took her left hand and slid it on her ring finger.

"Lily, he said, looking directly into her eyes, will you please marry me – ASAP"

With tears threatening to leak down her cheeks, Lily said, "Yes,

Richard Wadsworth Anderson I *will* marry you, and ASAP may not be soon enough for me."

Suddenly cheers broke out from behind her. Apparently Rick's family had not been engaged in things they had urgently needed to do. They had been lurking, and listening, behind a not so closed door. The whole thing had been a set-up. Lily reflected later that she had never been hugged so often, or so lovingly, by anyone, other than her own parents – ever before.

CHAPTER SEVENTEEN

Dangers Seen and Unseen

"Just because," Magnificence informed Andromeda, "the deceived one has been undeceived, does not mean the threat to the chosen ones is over."

"I assumed that would be the case," Andromeda replied, "that is the way of these things, have been since the rebellion of Lucifer, and the fall of humanity. Do you, however, have any specific information regarding this new threat our charges are facing?"

"You remember," Magnificence asked, "when I was summoned to a gathering of the great princes?"

"I do."

"It was revealed to me a new threat, arising from the original motivation of 'the deceived one,' is continuing against our charges. The threat has been designated as 'the imposter, a designation you will understand by the very form of the attack being made."

"You mean the one posing the threat is taking on the persona of someone they are not?"

"That is exactly what I mean, Andromeda. It is the old tactic the Serpent used when he deceived Adam and Eve in the Garden of Eden.

"And a very effective tactic it was, too."

"A very effective tactic it was indeed."

As it turned out, Lily did not have to work for more than a month of the three months agreed upon. She stayed a further two weeks to train the new secretary; not a chore, since Sarah Jameson was a bright and engaging young woman. She was also a quick study, picking up on routines and procedures Lily could not remember mastering as quickly herself.

More importantly, Sarah connected with all who approached her desk, dealt with their concerns efficiently, and left them smiling their appreciation for how she had served them. She was also avidly committed to her faith in Christ. She left Lily feeling her replacement was a grade above her own standards, and even of Carolyn herself. She was perfect. A thought crept into Lily's mind she rejected immediately: Sarah Jameson seemed almost *too* perfect.

"Lily, your wedding dress is *gorgeous*. You're going to look like a fairytale princess."

Lily viewed herself in the full-length mirror in her bedroom, doubtfully.

"Don't you think is a little retro?"

Heather cleared her throat dismissively, "Lily, of *course* your wedding dress is retro. Your mother wore it when she married your father over twenty years ago. That, however, is not the point. It is perfect for *you*. There are several points in its favour."

"And those are?"

"First, it is not going to cost you anything. Apart from a good dry-cleaning to restore its freshness, that is.

"Second, it's not going to need any alterations. It looks as if it was made and measured just for you. It's amazing."

"Actually," Lily said, going to her bureau drawer and retrieving a framed picture, my mother looked *just* like I do. Not her facial features exactly, though I do bear a resemblance to her. Our figures, however, appear to be identical."

"Just my point. There are other reasons why any other dress would be wrong for you."

"Okay, I'll bite. What are they?"

"Your mother would *want* you to wear it for your wedding."

"How in Heaven's name could you know that, Heather?"

"Just a strong suspicion, Lily, but I would lay a bet on it. If you asked your father he would tell you your mother told him it would please her if you did."

"I will ask him, so what else?"

"*You* want to wear that dress for your wedding, Lily."

"Now you're a mind reader, on top of all the other things you dream up in that imagination of yours."

"Deny it, Lily and I'll believe you. I've see the look on your face and the look in your eye when you look at yourself in that dress."

"Alright, I'll admit it. Something about wearing my mother's wedding dress feels special. You've convinced me, but I believe you have one more argument in favour of me wearing it."

"Your *father* would like you to wear it."

"Has he told you so?"

"Not in so many words, but I saw the look on his face when he gave it to you. Believe me, he *wants* you to wear this dress. He just does not want you to feel obligated to do so."

"So, it has been decided. I will be wearing my mother's wedding dress."

"I don't think you *needed* to be convinced, Lily. You were just being perverse, seeing how far you could push me."

"How did you know, Heather? It is so much fun pushing your buttons."

"Only best friends can do that to each other – and get away with it. And don't forget it, Lily Cameron – soon to be Anderson."

Sarah Jameson arrived home after her final day of orientation into her new position at Community Church.

She sat in her favourite chair and allowed herself to feel the warm glow of accomplishment. She was now in a position to achieve her aims, and exact the revenge she had dreamed about for over seven years.

She was, of course *not* Sarah Jameson, but Sarah's corpse had been officially identified as a different person entirely. She, the fake Sarah Jameson, was now officially dead. It was essential she not be identified as a relative of the family so tragically wiped out by Rick Anderson seven years ago. She had been content till now to let justice be exacted by another. By Andrew Wheller.

She and Roland Mills had supported Andrew in his endeavour to bring about justice for the death of her sister, her sister's husband, and their three little girls. The plan had been to exact an eye for an eye, and a tooth for a tooth. Or in this case, a death for a death. The plan included anyone who had been a close associate of the original killer, Rick Anderson. Lily Cameron, since she was marrying Rick, must also share the same fate as her soon to be husband.

The problem was, Andrew Wheller had gone soft. He planned to confess, not only to the two murder attempts, but of several undetected murders he had previously committed. Even Roland Mills had refused to be involved any more in exacting revenge for the death of her family members. Initially incensed at Andrew's intention to confess, he had changed his mind.

Influenced by Andrew's actions, he now planned to make a full confession to the police himself. Both he and Andrew were doing this in order to find God's forgiveness, the same God who had not prevented the senseless killing of her own family. She, the substitute Sarah Jameson, was not going to give up so easily. Rick, Lily, and possibly Heather Rawlings, would pay the ultimate price for the death of her family.

She would also dedicate herself to opposing and undermining the Gospel. It was the Gospel that proclaimed forgiveness for the worst of sinners. *No one* deserved forgiveness for such sins as Rick Anderson had committed against her family. She would fight any religion that proclaimed that they did.

The Pastor responsible for student admissions, prepared himself to process letters of application.

He set aside those wanting to become pastors, and those just wanting to enhance their Bible knowledge. What was left on his desk was a small pile of applications for the missionary service course of study. These he quickly processed till he came to the last one. His secretary had paper-clipped another letter to it, as if it was somehow related.

He withdrew the letter his secretary had marked 'anonymous' first.

I just wanted, the letter read, *"to warn you concerning two applicants who are applying to attend your college. They are less than qualified for the course of study they are applying for.*

Their names are Lily Cameron and Richard Anderson. They are soon to be married and intend to attend your college as husband and wife. They have been involved in a scandal here in St. Catharines, and I am concerned they may bring disrepute to your college if they are allowed to attend.

I enclose some pictures distributed to all the churches in this area, which caused Lily Cameron to be dismissed from her secretarial position at the Community Church here.

For personal reasons I prefer to remain anonymous, but I trust this communication will result in preserving the testimony of your school.

With best wishes.

Laying that letter aside he examined the application of those the letter referred to and found the two superbly qualified. For one thing he knew the reputation of the girl's father, and co-signer of the application. For another he had read the editorial in a St. Catharine's newspaper, clearing the couple of all blame. His secretary had received a copy of the newspaper from her sister who lived there, and laid it on his desk.

He also knew Pastor Jake of the Community Church. He placed a call, and heard from him a clear account of what had *really* happened.

After replacing the receiver he called his secretary and got her to draft a letter of acceptance to the couple mentioned in the anonymous communication.

It always amazed him the lengths to which some people would go to besmirch the name of those with whom they disagreed. They completely missed the lengths to which the *Lord* will go to protect those who love Him.

Lily peered through the chapel window at what appeared to be a vast crowd gathered on the lawn outside.

She and Rick had intended to have only a small gathering, one that the small church recently relocated to *Balls Falls* was sufficient to host.

"It appeared, however, that the entire congregation of Pastor Jake's church, had had other ideas. They had covered the cost of the reception and the Mission Board had committed to covering the cost of college for the next three years. Lily found the whole thing overwhelming.

The bridal party, including Heather as her maid of honour, were to proceed down the front steps of the church to the lawn outside, where a portable pulpit had been set up. An archway, adorned with white flowers stood before the pulpit for the bridal couple to perform their vows.

The weather had co-operated, and, at the edge of the crowd, Lily could see trestle tables laden with food. And then Lily saw her groom waiting for her under the archway. After that she saw nothing but the man with whom she was going to spend the rest of her life. She was no longer to be known as Lily Cameron, but *Mrs.* Lily Anderson.

As her father placed her hand into that of her groom she felt like she was about to step into an entirely new world. In reality, she was doing exactly that.

It was like a dream till at last Pastor Jake said, "I now pronounce you husband and wife." Addressing Rick, he said, "You may now kiss your bride." The very first kiss as a married woman. A kiss that promised many, many more to come.

The reception seemed to go on forever, and at the end of it both she and Rick felt utterly exhausted.

Pastor Jake made a congratulatory speech, followed by a dozen more speeches from friends and well-wishers. After that everyone wanted to shake their hands. Lily knew from the attendance records there were well over a thousand in attendance.

All of the activity, and the highly emotional nature of the event, prevented either Lily or her new husband, from seeing, or feeling, the malicious glare directed at them the entire time. If looks could kill, as the saying goes – they would both of them have been dead. They were unaware their murder was being plotted – in meticulous detail. In the mind of this enemy, they would die an excruciating death – even if it took years to accomplish.

In the heavens a conversation was taking place that the malicious observer would not have believed if she had heard it with her own ears:

"Such hatred and evil intent, deserves only God's judgment," Andromeda said.

"Andromeda," Magnificence replied, *"you still do not yet comprehend the love God has for fallen humanity. He declares in His Word that he is not willing that any of them should perish, but that they all should come to repentance."*

"I confess that I do not understand such love, Magnificence, and I am certain you do not understand it yourself."

"Indeed I do not, but I do not think we angels are able to understand it. The closest we can come to understanding, is to bring to mind what the Son suffered on the cross to redeem them."

"So, you are saying this hateful person, with murder in her heart, is going to repent and be a recipient of God's mercy and forgiveness??

"I am not sure, Andromeda, but from what I have witnessed over the millennia, she just may be."

THE END

REFERENCES

[1] *(Isaiah58:8-9 – ESV)*
[2] *(Luke 1:51-53 KJV)*
[3] *(Isaiah 21:10 – ESV)*
[4] (Daniel 4:24-27 – ESV)
[5] *(Ephesians 6:12 – ESV)*
[6] *(Isaiah 41:10-13 – ESV*
[7] *(James 4:7-8a – ESV)*
[8] *(Zechariah 4:6b – ESV)*
[9] *(Matthew 27:41-44 – ESV)*
[10] *(Luke 23:39-41 – ESV)*
[11] *(Matthew 10:32-33 – ESV)*
[12] *(Luke 9:26 – ESV)*
[13]
[14] *(Ephesians 6:12 – ESV)*
[15] *(Ephesians 6:12 – ESV)*
[16] *(Acts 18:24-26 – ESV)*
[17] *(Ephesians 5:25 – ESV)*

Printed in the United States
By Bookmasters